AVOIDING TEMPTATION

FORBIDDEN SERIES #6

TRACY LORRAINE

A NOTE

Avoiding Temptation is written in British English and contains British spelling and grammar. This may appear incorrect to some readers when compared to US English books.

CHAPTER ONE

"YOU ALL SET?" Eddie asks, glancing at the first slide of my presentation projecting on the wall and to my neatly stacked folders and worksheets.

Tonight is my first class at my new job. I've been an English teacher since I graduated from university eight years ago, although I'm more used to teenagers than adults, but I didn't have the time or money to be fussy when I moved to London. I almost snapped Eddie's hand off when he offered me this position.

He's the only person I know in this city. I knew it was a risk going to him, but he was my only option. Thankfully, he was still at the same address he gave me years ago, and when he unlocked his front door he welcomed me in like it was only yesterday we'd last seen each other.

"Yeah, I think so." I shake my arms at my sides, willing my nerves to disappear before my students arrive. I don't need them figuring out my weakness the moment they walk in the room. The thought of teaching adults terrifies me, even if they've made the decision to better themselves. Put me in an entire hall full of teenagers and I wouldn't bat an eyelid, but adults are a whole other story.

"You're going to be fine. This'll be a walk in the park after the spoilt rich kids you're used to."

"If you say so."

The classroom door opens and both Eddie and I look over. It takes a couple of seconds for someone to enter but, when they do, my chin drops a little. I didn't have any expectations of who my students might be. Eddie explained to me that the classes are usually a total mixed bag of people, but I can say with absolute certainty that I was not expecting someone like him.

His eyes find mine briefly before he looks away to take in the room. With his head down, he walks to the back and takes a seat in the last row. It gives me time to assess him. His eyes are hiding behind thick-rimmed glasses, but it's his outfit that really catches my attention. His white dress shirt is perfectly pressed, stretched across his wide shoulders and rolled up to the elbows exposing muscular forearms covered in tattoos. The black braces that sit over his shoulders make the corner of my mouth twitch up. Although his demeanor right now doesn't show it, I've no doubt that on a normal day this man is full of confidence.

"Told you, all walks of life in this place." Eddie's obvious distaste for the man at the back of the room drips from him, reminding me that although he's here helping me, he's still firmly from my old life. "Probably part of his rehabilitation or something."

Feeling eyes on me, I turn back to look at the guy, who's now staring right at us. His previous hesitant look seems to have vanished as his eyes drop from mine in favour of my body.

My skin tingles with his attention. I can't lie, it's a good feeling after being practically invisible for so long, but this is neither the time nor the place.

After lingering on my leather skirt for a few seconds too long, his eyes find mine once again. The brightness of his blue irises makes my breath catch. Surely they're not real?

A commotion at the door forces us to break our connection as others enter.

"Time to get to work, Miss Smith." Eddie winks before lifting his knuckles to my cheek. "No need to look so worried. I couldn't think of anyone better for the job."

His eyes bore down into mine and my stomach twists. I assumed Eddie would have a girlfriend by now. He's a great guy, but it was immediately obvious that he was still living life as a bachelor after he invited me to his flat when I turned up on his doorstep. He's been an amazing friend, more so than I think he knows, but that's all there's ever going to be between us. I'm just not attracted to him like I think he wants me to be. Although he didn't really fit in my past life, hence why he moved on a few years ago, he still reminds me of everything I hated about it. He still wears the flashy suit with the pretentious pocket square and tie pin. I've had enough of all of that shit for a lifetime. If there's ever going to be another man in my life, I want him to be as different from what I've known previously as possible.

"Thank you. You'd better go before you're late for class."

He nods before mouthing good luck and

stepping away from me, and I feel like I can breathe again. He's been the perfect gentleman and friend since I arrived, but I fear he might be expecting too much. I'd hate to hurt him after everything he's done for me.

Just before he walks out of my classroom, he looks back over his shoulder, and my stomach drops at the twinkle in his eye. I'm sure it works on other women—unfortunately for him, I'm not them.

When I look back towards the desks facing me, I see that they're almost all full. Doing a quick head count, I realise we're still missing a couple. "We'll give it another two minutes, and then we'll get started."

I spend most of the first lesson outlining what they can expect from the course, the kind of assignments they're going to have to complete, and which books we're going to be studying. It's weird, because although everyone here is much older than I'm used to, I still see the same stereotypical students. At the front are two women who look overly keen to learn—it makes me wonder why they need to re-do this qualification if they're so enthusiastic. Behind them are a few rows of what I'd class as average students who follow all instructions to a tee, followed by a couple of guys in suits who, although they do what I tell them to, look like they want to be anywhere but here. Then of course, there's *him* at the back. The man who, every time I look up, I find staring right at me.

With only ten minutes left, I set them all a quick task to write a poem like the one they've been analysing that will help me get to know them.

Everyone puts their heads down and gets to work, aside from him. His eyes follow me as I walk to my desk and pick up the stack of folders. A shiver runs down my spine as his attention holds. He's the kind of guy I dreamt of running away with when I was a teenager, if I ever had the chance. I wanted the bad boy to rescue me from my life of china tea cups and pearls. It never happened, and, as was inevitable, I'd ended up becoming one of them. If only I'd had the strength to get out sooner.

I drop a folder on everyone's desk and ask each student if they have any questions or concerns about what we've done so far. I can only imagine their heads must be spinning, especially if they haven't been in education for a while.

Swallowing my trepidation, I step up to his desk and drop a folder.

"How are you doing?" I glance at his still blank page. "Is there anything I can do to help?"

He drops his pen on top of his paper haphazardly, and my fingers twitch to straighten it as he sits back. His eyes crawl up my body until they find mine. The blue is even more striking up close.

"I'm sure there's plenty you could help me with, Miss Smith." His eyes flit around my face, and there's no way he misses the brightening of my cheeks. My temperature begins to increase the longer he stares at me, and I know that I need to walk away—only, my legs don't seem to want to cooperate.

"So, tell me...will you be our teacher every Thursday night?"

"I would think so, yes. Problem?"

"Oh no. That is most definitely not a problem."

"Brilliant. Any concerns about the course or the work...Joe?" I ask, glancing at the name he's written on one of the forms I'd given him.

He shakes his head, and finally my legs allow me to get the hell away from him.

The second I dismiss the class, everyone starts moving, some faster and keener to get away than others.

"How'd it go?" Eddie asks, slipping inside the room when there's a break in students leaving.

"It was good. I'm not sure I'm ever going to be able to thank you enough for this."

"No need. When our new appointment decided against the position after his first day, we were pretty stuck. We should be thanking you for turning up when you did."

A chair scratching across the wooden floor makes both Eddie and I wince. Turning, we both watch as Joe collects up his stuff.

"Great class, Miss Smith. Very...inspirational." He winks, and I want the ground to swallow me up.

"Please, call me Quinn. This isn't school."

"Sure thing, Quinn." The way my name sounds rolling off his tongue has tingles erupting in my belly. "Already looking forward to next week." With a nod of his head, he drops his books into his bag and heads for the door.

"Looks like you've already got yourself a pet." The way Eddie's lips curl up in disgust as he watches Joe leave ignites a fire in my belly. I thought I'd left all the judgemental arseholes behind. "Lift home?"

I want to say no after that last comment, but

the thought of navigating through London on a cold and dark winter night fills me with dread. I'm sure it'll feel like second nature soon, but right now, I don't feel like I belong, let alone know where I'm going. I begrudgingly agree and start to gather up my things.

"Still think you made the right decision?" Eddie asks once we're on the road. His eyes flick over to me every few minutes, and I wish he'd just focus on the road ahead.

"Most definitely. I just can't wait for this place to feel like home."

"It won't take long. You fancy going for a drink?"

"Um...can I call a rain check tonight? I'd really like to be prepared for tomorrow, if that's okay?" I hate saying no after everything he's done for me recently, but I can't help feeling like agreeing would be giving him the wrong idea.

"No, that's fine. I totally get it. I know I've thrown you in at the deep end. I'm not taking no for an answer tomorrow night, though. I'm on the VIP list for one of the best clubs around, and I want to show you what London really has to offer."

"I...uh..." The thought of being thrust into London's thriving nightlife kind of terrifies me.

Well, it terrifies the old me. I need to remember that she's long gone. The girl sitting here right now is ready to start experiencing life, start living it to the fullest and taking some risks. Suddenly, a little excitement I remember when I first got here tingles in my belly. "Yes. I'd love to."

"Get out your best dress, Quinn. I'm going to show you how it's really done."

Dress. Shit.

I school my features before thanking him for the ride and jumping from the car.

I make quick work of getting inside my building and up the stairs to the studio flat Eddie helped me find.

The small space is nothing like I'm used to, but, for the first time in my life, it's *my* space. It might be tiny, but it's mine to do with as I wish. Well...as long as the landlord agrees. I've wanted my own life for as long as I can remember, and I'm finally here.

I drop my bags onto the small coffee table that sits in front of my sofa bed and head towards the kitchen for a glass of water. I down it before popping a couple of slices of bread into the grill for dinner. I might have my own life now, but, at least until I get paid, it's not exactly what my dreams were made of.

Once I've stripped out of my jumper and skirt, I pull on an old pair of pyjamas and stare at the number of items I've got hanging in my wardrobe.

I left my previous life with only a handful of essentials. I hated the majority of my clothes; they represented a life I hated. The first thing I did when I arrived here was head to a shop and purchase a couple of items I'd always wanted to own. The knee-high boots and short leather skirt I've just taken off were two of those items. Looks like I'm going to have to hit the shops again if I need something for a night out tomorrow.

I spend the night working on lesson plans and, sometime after midnight, flip my sofa to a bed and curl up under the blanket.

My flat might be cold, and I might not have much in the way of possessions, but I still fall asleep with a smile on my face because this life right now is everything I've ever wanted.

CHAPTER TWO

"WHOA THIS PLACE LOOKS...FANCY," I say as I walk beside Eddie towards the club he's spent almost all day telling me about. Suddenly, the little black Primark dress I thought looked pretty hot when I was in the fitting room first thing this morning doesn't seem good enough.

Looking down, I run my palm over the figure-hugging fabric and let out a sigh.

"You look stunning," Eddie whispers, assuming correctly where my thoughts are at. "That look suits you much better than the twinsets I'd become used to."

"Thanks," I mutter, but when I glance up, I see a little fire in his eyes as he drops them down my body. I stand up a little straighter. I don't want him looking at me that way, but if he is, then it must mean I don't stand out like an outsider trying to force my way into a new life.

Eddie walks straight up to the bouncer and gives him his name. Glancing over my shoulder, I take in the long line of people waiting to get in. This place, The Avenue, is clearly popular, and I can't help yearning to be part of that crowd. It might sound crazy because almost anyone would love to be in my position now, being waved through to go to the VIP section, but all I want is a normal life. I want to blend in with the crowd and disappear.

"Come on," Eddie says, grabbing my hand and pulling me towards him when he realises that I'm not following. "What's wrong? You want to join the peasants?"

His words have anger burning in my stomach. Does he really think he's so special? Pulling my hand from his, I follow him up the stairs to the second floor before we walk around the edge of the vast room to another set of stairs that are guarded by security and sectioned off with a red rope. The music is so loud, it vibrates through my bones, but I can't deny that it doesn't make me want to dance.

Eddie speaks to the bouncer as if he's a regular

—which he probably is—giving me a chance to look around.

I've always wondered if clubs are like they're portrayed on the TV, and standing here right now I can confidently say yes. Everything about this place is exactly what I was expecting. Its floors are polished black with silver flecks, and all the fittings are chrome with huge glass chandeliers hanging from the high ceilings. The bar is packed, the queue of people at least five deep as they wait a little impatiently for their next drink. But the majority of the room is given over to a dance floor where hundreds of bodies move and gyrate to the beat.

I'm totally lost watching their movement when Eddie slips his arm around my waist and moves me towards the stairs.

"We can dance later if you like. I need a few drinks first to loosen up a little."

A shudder runs down my spine. I'm not sure I want him loosened up. He's free enough with his hands as it is.

Gritting my teeth and fighting my need to step away from his touch, I allow him to guide me up to the bar.

The difference in the clientele up here is stark,

and it only increases my desire to go back down and mix with the masses. I look around at the designer suits and fancy dresses, and it's just like being in the middle of my old life where everyone's biggest concern was how they looked and how much money they had.

Eddie leans over when the barman comes over. At no point does he look back to ask what I want, which irritates the hell out of me. I know he's been my confidant over the past few years, but he couldn't possibly know what I want to drink right now.

It's only a few seconds later when I realise why he didn't bother asking, because the barman reappears with a bottle of champagne and two glasses. Eddie hands over his credit card before grabbing his purchase and leading me over to the balcony. He places the glasses down on one of the high tables and pulls over two stools for us to sit on. Glad to have some space, I pull the stool a little closer to the glass balcony that allows us to look down over the dancefloor below.

It's like I blink and there's a glass of champagne shoved under my nose. I guess now wouldn't be the best time to tell him that I don't really like the stuff.

"To new starts, new jobs, and...friendships."

His eyes twinkle as he says the final word. "I'm so glad you reached out when you did. I think this is where you're meant to be."

"Eddie, I—" I'm just about to explain to him that there's not going to be anything between us when someone approaches and holds their hand out for him to shake.

The two men start talking like they're old friends—it's not lost on me that at no point does Eddie bother to introduce me. Clearly, I'm not that important.

Ignoring them, I take a sip of champagne and try not to turn my nose up too much. I really shouldn't complain; it's not like I can afford to buy my own drinks in a place like this. I dread to think how much this bottle cost. It seems that Eddie could take himself out of my old stuck-up and pretentious life, but he couldn't remove his inner snob.

Rolling my eyes at my thoughts, I look down over the mass of bodies below. They've all got smiles on their faces as they dance and laugh with friends, and my muscles ache to know how that feels. Eddie is the closest thing I've had to a proper friend since I was a child. The thought makes my stomach drop. I'd kill to have a girlfriend to share everything with, to go shopping with and share my dreams and fears. I had that when I was a kid, but Suzi ended up moving to the States with her parents not long after we finished school, and the distance between us put pay to our friendship.

I let out a sigh as I once again think about what a lonely life I've lived up until this point. The knowledge that I've done something about it at last has a little hope starting to filter into my depressing thoughts.

I'm not all that different to the adults I've started teaching. For whatever reason, they've all decided that now's the time to better themselves. I might not need qualifications like them, but I am in need of other things. I just hope that I'm able to find what's missing in my life in my new home, and I don't end up going back to where I came from with my tail between my legs, just like I'm sure they're all expecting me to do.

Someone's exuberant dancing below catches my eye. I have to do a double-take when a familiar figure comes into focus.

It's the guy who sat at the back of my room yesterday evening. He's dressed similarly, only his white shirt is grey tonight, his braces firmly in place over the top, and his thick-rimmed glasses sit on his face. That's where the similarities end, because where he was a little unsure of himself last night, right now he's full of confidence as he dances with a group of friends.

I can't pull my eyes away as he pulls a petite redhead into his body and wraps his tattooed arms around her waist. Their hips move together in time with the music. They're so in sync they could be making love.

Jealousy hits me like a truck. It's not because I want to be the redhead—I don't think—but because I want that connection with someone. I want my body to connect with someone else's so easily that I don't even need to think about it.

I find myself downing the glass in my hand, needing something to dampen the emotion bubbling up my throat. I continue watching and, before long, he spins the redhead away from him and pulls the equally tattooed man standing to the side of him to dance.

Oh...

He moves as effortlessly with him as he did with the girl, and it only sparks even more questions about my elusive nerdy bad boy student.

The other guy soon gets fed up and, with a laugh, pushes Joe away and pulls a girl into his body before shoving his tongue down her throat. When I eventually drag my voyeuristic eyes away from the couple, I find Joe sandwiched between another guy and a girl. The girl's at his front, Joe's hands roaming over her body as her head rolls back in pleasure, but what really holds my attention is that his lips are attached to the guy's. They kiss like they'll die without it, and I can't pull my eyes away.

Something inside me erupts, lust descending to my core like I've never felt before. I've no idea if it's him, him and the guy, or just the three of them together, but fuck, it's hot.

"Jesus, don't they have any morals? It's embarrassing," Eddie tuts, following my stare.

"They're just letting their hair down and enjoying themselves."

"They might as well just fuck each other while everyone watches." I glance up at him through narrowed eyes before finding Joe again. "What? Don't tell me that you'd rather be down in the middle of that than up here with me?" He hands me a refilled glass as if I should be impressed by the expensive golden liquid I'm supposed to be enjoying.

I don't respond, knowing that he wouldn't like or understand my answer, because, yes, yes I really do want to be down there in the middle of all that. I want to experience everything I've missed out on with my sheltered life. I want to act wild, to do things my parents would be ashamed of but what normal young people do on a weekly basis.

Eddie manages to drag me away from my spot looking down over the fun below in favour of introducing me to some of his friends. I take one look at their designer suits, handbags and botox, and I know that I'm not about to be making friends with any of them.

I try to smile and nod at all the right times, but aside from being in a different location, I may as well be back in my old life. This is the kind of pretentious bullshit I was desperate to get away from.

My imagination sees me through the rest of the night, and, by my fourth glass of champagne, I've almost plucked up the courage to abandon Eddie and his self-obsessed friends in favour of finding my own fun. But just as I've decided to excuse myself to the toilets, his hand lands on the small of my back.

"You ready to get out of here?"

A little disappointment settles in my belly, knowing that I missed my opportunity to escape.

But am I ready to get out of here? Yes. I was from the moment he directed me up to the VIP area.

———

EDDIE QUICKLY FINDS the taxi he'd ordered and ushers me inside. He slides across the seat until he's sitting a little too close and, after barking my address at the driver, turns his heated stare on me.

"This place suits you." His fingers capture a lock of my short black hair as his eyes flit around my face. He knew me in my previous life as a blonde. The first thing I did when I left, before I even got to his place, was find a hairdresser. Gone are my long, golden locks in favour of a short, dark bob. I'd always thought I'd suit short hair, and the excitement I felt at being able to experiment almost got the better of me as I sat in that chair, my head spinning with delight.

"T-thank you."

It amazes me that he doesn't mention the other —what I would think is obvious—change, but he seems to have forgotten what colour my eyes were when we first met.

"I missed you when I left. I thought of you

often and whether or not I should have come back for you."

"That wasn't for you to decide. I needed to wait until the time was right. You'd already caused me enough drama." I laugh, but it's anything but amused and more clipped and uncomfortable as he edges even closer.

"We could be really good, you and me, *Quinn*." The emphasis he puts on my name makes a shudder run down my spine.

"I'm not sure that's such a good idea."

"Why not? You came to me for help. You must have known I'd want more with this second chance."

Lifting my hand, I place it on his chest in an attempt to make him back off a little.

"You're my friend, Eddie. I appreciate our relationship more than you could know. But that's all it is. You know what I've left behind and must be able to understand that I just need to be me for a little while."

"But—"

"No buts. I came here for me...not for you. I came to you as my friend, as someone who could help me. That's what I need right now. A friend. Can you be that?" I ask, my voice stronger than I thought it would be when I was brave enough to have this conversation with him.

His eyes bounce between mine as if he's waiting for me to tell him I'm joking. But I'm not. I'm deadly serious. Eddie's been a really good friend since the day I met him, but that's all we're ever going to be.

The taxi slows to a stop, and, when I drag my eyes from Eddie, I find we're outside my building.

"Thank you for a nice night. I'll see you at work next week."

"You sure you don't want me to walk you up?"

I look around at the dark and deserted car park, my heart starting to race a little, but I refuse to give him the wrong idea, even if he only does mean well. "No, I'll be fine. See you soon."

Before he can argue, I hop out of the taxi and all but run towards the front door. I know I'm safe here, but it doesn't stop me looking over my shoulder, especially at night.

CHAPTER THREE

BUTTERFLIES FLUTTER in my belly as my Thursday night class starts to filter into my classroom. Tonight marks a week at my new job, and although it's very different to my previous teaching position, I'm quite enjoying it. There's something so easy and relaxed about teaching adults who mostly want to be here. It's miles away from the privileged kids I'm used to.

Each student finds their seat and pulls out the folder I gave them last week, ready to get to work, but the desk at the back remains empty. I try not to dwell on the fact that I was kind of looking forward to seeing him again after the show on Friday night, but it's there nonetheless.

It's two minutes after the lesson is meant to

begin, and he's still not arrived. Pushing him from my mind, I address the class and get started.

I've just about finished explaining what I'd like them all to do when the door flies open and crashes back against the wall. Everyone in the room turns to see what's going on, but his eyes only find mine. Our contact holds for a few seconds too long before he breaks away in favour of finding his seat.

"Nice of you to join us, Mr. Kingsman." He tips his chin, telling me that he heard, but he still remains mute as he falls down onto his chair. He doesn't bother pulling anything from his bag, causing anger to erupt in my belly. What was I saying about the difference between teaching adults and teenagers? This defiance is something I'm much more used to.

"Don't worry, Miss Smith. I never stand up a good-looking woman." He winks, and my breath catches in my throat.

Fuck.

A gasp echoes around the room.

"Right. Well. In case you hadn't noticed, this is school, and your lack of punctuality won't be tolerated."

"I'm sure I have a few ways to ensure it's overlooked."

"Good for you." Picking up the worksheet he should be making a start on like some of the less nosey members of the class, I walk towards him.

Picking up his bag, I make a show of dropping it to the floor with a thud before pushing his foot from the top of the desk. "This is evening school, Mr. Kingsman, not primary school. I suggest you start acting appropriately. I'll catch you up on what you missed after class seeing as you couldn't get yourself here on time." I give him some very short and sharp instructions before turning and walking away, hoping to find some air to drag into my lungs.

I spend the rest of the class trying to ignore his piercing stare from the back of the room and the fact that whenever he's finished a task I've given him, he puts his feet up on the desk. He's baiting me, I'm aware of that, but I'm falling for it hook, line and sinker.

Everyone else is still reading through the first two chapters of 'Romeo and Juliet', ready to discuss it, but even with my head down, looking at my planner for this week's homework assignment, I can feel his stare.

Unable to resist the urge to find out what it is he wants, I lift my eyes.

A smug smile tugs at the corner of his lips in accomplishment.

Damn him.

Like he knows exactly how to wind me up, he makes a show of screwing up a piece of paper from his pad and making a half-arsed attempt at launching it towards the bin.

I fight my need to look at where it actually lands and put it in the bin where it should be. I'm strong for a few minutes, but eventually my desire for everything to be in the right place gets the better of me. As I'm summing up what the students should have just read, I bend down, pick it up and drop it in the bin. I feel his amusement behind me, and, when I turn around, I'm proved right when I see a wide smile on his face.

Arsehole.

"And make sure you're all on time next week," I call after I've finished going over their assignment. A couple of sniggers fill the room as all but one of the students put their stuff away and leave the room.

Joe, on the other hand, puts his feet back up on the desk and crosses his arms over his chest.

My teeth grind as I stare at him. The fabric of his shirt strains under his muscular arms and across his wide chest. I take in the ink covering his forearms, and my stomach clenches as I wonder how many others his clothes could be hiding.

I came to London with the intention of doing all the things I've craved since I was old enough to appreciate what a sheltered life I'd led. I wanted to be my own boss, wear clothes that I wanted and listen to the music I loved. Nowhere on my list was to be tempted by a bad boy, but shit, if he isn't exactly what I need after the boring, vanilla life I've led. I've no doubt that he'd help me break all the rules I've been forced to live my life by.

His eyebrow lifts as if he's waiting for me to do something, and before I think against it, I stalk towards his desk, place my palms on the smooth surface beside his feet, and stare deep into his eyes. Just like with a teenager, he needs to know I won't cower down to him.

"I'm still waiting for an apology for being late, Mr. Kingsman."

Unfolding his hands, he reaches for a pen that's lying haphazardly on his desk. Lifting it to his mouth, he taps a couple of times and, just like he probably planned, my eyes zero in on his full, soft looking lips.

My mouth waters, and I swallow as I fight to

remove the inappropriate images playing out in my head.

When his eyes drop from holding mine captive to my cleavage, I almost stand, horrified that I've put myself on show like that in front of a student. But he's not just a student. He's the kind of guy I've been dreaming about since I discovered them. He's the bad boy I've imagined running away with a million times, and, with the way he's biting down on his lip right now, I'd say his thoughts aren't too opposite to my own. A bolt of excitement races through me about how wrong this is. Anyone could walk through the door any moment and find me giving my student an eyefull.

My temperature spikes, and my breasts swell under his gaze. Thank fuck for padded bras.

Bending down, I bring myself so we're at the same height and force his eyes back to mine.

The bright blue that has been staring back at me for the past two hours is significantly darker, almost black.

Clearing my throat, I start to explain what it was he missed when he decided to turn up almost twenty minutes late. "So, as you've probably now figured out, we're going to be studying 'Romeo and—'"

"Quinn, are you ready?" Eddie calls from the doorway. "Oh, sorry. I didn't realise you were running a late session." His eyes bounce between the two of us, deep lines forming across his forehead.

"I'm not. I'm just catching Joe up on what he missed as he was a little la—"

"Lateness will not be tolerated around here," Eddie barks, his angry stare homing in on Joe. "If it happens again, I will be forced to reevaluate your position on this course."

"Fantastic," Joe mutters under his breath, making me chuckle to myself. Why am I not surprised that this man isn't even a little concerned that someone of authority is giving him a dressing down?

He slips his feet from the desk, collects his stuff and shoves it all into his bag. My fingers twitch to reach out and arrange it inside properly, but that's none of my business, even if the pages of 'Romeo and Juliet' are now getting dog-eared. I shudder at the thought and rise to full height.

"We've got reservations. Are you ready?" Eddie eventually says, turning his heated stare from Joe to me.

"Y-yes. Let me grab my bag."

I quickly swipe a Post-it Note from my desk and scribble my email address down.

"Mr. Kingsman, any questions, just shoot me an email. I'll see you next week."

He shrugs on a leather jacket before throwing his bag across his body, nods in my direction, and takes a step to leave. His eyes stay locked on mine the entire time, ensuring that the tingles he initiated earlier continue to simmer just under the surface. I sense Eddie looking between us, and eventually I manage to pull my eyes away.

Pulling my own bag over my shoulder, I walk over to Eddie. "Be careful, Quinn. That one's got trouble written all over him."

"Don't worry. I've handled worse."

"I know. I've met them," he says sadly. Unfortunately, he's right, and I know he's not necessarily talking about my past students.

He takes me to a Chinese place not far from my flat. Thankfully, after my little speech in the taxi last week, he seems to have backed off a little.

"So what's that guy's story then?" he asks once we've ordered.

My heart starts to race at just the mention of him. "No idea. You probably know more about him than me, seeing as you'd have processed his application, right?" Eddie is head of department at the college, so I'm assuming part of his job is vetting applicants.

"I guess I did. Sadly, they aren't required to supply a selfie."

Anger twists my stomach that he's once again judging him based on his tattoos and style.

"He might be the brightest student in that class. How he looks has nothing to do with it."

"But what kind of job will he ever get, looking like that?"

"Plenty. Tattoos can be covered, Eddie. Bad attitudes are harder to hide," I mutter to myself, but, by the narrowing of his eyes, I know he heard me.

We have a nice enough night, but at no point can I forget about the judgmental side of him that he's too quick to show. Maybe it's always been there, but because previously we were surrounded by people who were much, much worse, it wasn't so obvious. But now I've removed myself from that life, I want all of it gone, and I'm afraid that Eddie is going to be part of that unless he fixes his attitude.

It's not until I've securely locked myself inside

my flat later that night that I pull my phone from my bag.

It's nothing special, just the cheapest smartphone I could find when I first arrived, but it does the job.

No one aside from Eddie has this number, and only one other person knows where I was headed, so I'm a little surprised when I find a notification for an email when the screen lights up.

To: Quinn Smith
From: Tatstwatsandarseholes
Subject: Romeo seeks Juliet

Dear Miss Smith,
I sincerely hope you had a wonderful evening with
Mr. Boring, although I can't imagine he fulfilled all
of your desires.
I wanted to thank you for taking the time to go
through our current assignment with me seeing as I
was so rudely late to class. I can assure you that it
won't happen again.
I always come on time.
Yours,
Joe Kingsman

I stare down at my phone with my eyes wide and my mouth gaping open. Did one of my students just tell me he comes on demand?

What the hell have I got myself into here? My temperature spikes as I begin to type a reply.

To: *Tatstwatsandarseholes*

Who in god's name has an email like that?

From: *Quinn Smith*
Subject: *Romeo needs to work harder*

Dear Mr, Kingsman,
I'm glad I could be of assistance. Any problems
with the work, please don't hesitate to ask.
Regards,
Miss Smith
PS. My evening was...boring.

The wine Eddie ordered us is clearly having an effect, because before I've really thought about it I hit send. I regret it instantly. What the hell am I doing, and why am I more excited right now than I've ever been in my life?

The screen lights up.

To: *Quinn Smith*
From: *Tatstwatsandarseholes*
Subject: *Juliet deserves more*

Dear Miss Smith,
I think you need some excitement in your life, and I know just where you can find it...
Very much looking forward to our next lesson.
Mr. Kingsman

With a smile spreading across my lips, I close down my email app and silence my phone. This has already gone too far. The moment I didn't move when I knew he was checking out my cleavage was a step over the line, but this? This is way beyond the kind of rule breaking and excitement I was looking for.

CHAPTER FOUR

I'VE NEVER BEEN this nervous to start a class, but when my Thursday night students begin entering the room, my whole body is vibrating with anxiety.

I knew I shouldn't have replied to his inappropriate email last week, but I couldn't help myself. He's just too tempting with the bad boy geek look he's got going on. It calls to the wild side this boring English teacher has kept hidden for most of her life.

I expect him to be late just to push my buttons again, but it seems he took his warning from Eddie seriously, because he's the fourth student to enter.

I follow his movements as he walks towards his normal desk and pulls out his folder, pad of paper and pens. Then he just sits and waits as everyone else gets themselves ready. At no point does he look up, and it annoys the shit out of me that I've been so worried about seeing him all day, and he's totally indifferent.

My nerves give way to shame and embarrassment as I think about how easily I played his game, because clearly that was all this was to him.

I welcome the class and set them up on the first activity, which is to be done in pairs.

Sitting down behind my desk, I watch as they all move closer to their allocated partner and begin their discussions, but before long my eyes find their way back to him and the woman he's working with.

The second I look up, I meet his blue eyes. My breath catches as a smirk spreads across his face before he turns his attention back to her.

Tingles erupt and my thighs clench. It's not the reaction to a student I should be having, but my body doesn't seem to care as I fight to drag my eyes away from where he's leaning into his partner and absorbing every word she's saying.

The next thirty minutes of my life are possibly some of the most frustrating I've ever experienced. No matter how hard I try, I can't stop myself from glancing up at them, and every time I do, I regret it. It's like he knows and intentionally does something to wind me up.

His partner is young, and even I can admit how pretty she is. He makes sure that both she and I know it. He runs the back of his knuckles up her arm, tucking a lock of hair behind her ear when they're both looking down and studying the text I've given them. He laughs animatedly in a way I'm sure isn't all that natural when she says something. And although I'm pretty convinced he's acting for my benefit, it hits the exact spot he was intending.

It's infuriating. *He's* infuriating.

Once they all return to their own seats, Joe goes back to ignoring me. It's much easier to deal with, but the nagging need to make him look up at me gets more and more impossible to ignore.

There's only ten minutes left of the lesson, and I'm walking around, collecting what everyone's been doing so I can mark it, when the sound of a pencil dropping on the floor in front of me catches my attention. I step towards it, my need to have everything just so too much to ignore, and just as I'm about to bend, someone shifts behind me. It's only then that I realise this is a game, and I have a millisecond to decide if I'm going to play on the wild side.

Moving here was all about pushing boundaries.

In a moment of madness, I bend over and pick up the pencil. Excitement fills my veins, knowing that I shouldn't be joining in with his games, but I can't help myself. My stomach clenches at the thought of someone watching me openly flirt, but the risk isn't enough to stop me.

I slowly turn and place the pencil back onto his desk, lining it up perfectly alongside his paper. Risking a look at his face, my breath catches when I find his dark eyes and his teeth digging into his bottom lip.

Every muscle in my body freezes as his eyes drop from mine in favour of taking a leisurely stroll around my body. I'm dressed differently this week, seeing as I haven't been able to get to the laundrette yet, so my old trusty twinset and a-line skirt have sadly made a reappearance.

Desire still fills his eyes, but when he opens his mouth, something else entirely comes out. "Mr. Boring rubbing off on you, teach? Didn't have you down as a cardigan and pearl necklace type."

My shoulders stiffen at the reference to my old life, although I'm equally as glad I've managed to pull off my new persona as I am frustrated that he's noticed the change.

"Don't always judge a book by its cover, Mr. Kingsman."

"I'm beginning to learn that, Miss Smith."

When I eventually pull my eyes from his and glance to the clock on the wall, I notice that we're about to run over.

"Right, well. Looks like we're done for the day. I'll have all these marked for you for next week. Any questions about this week's assignment, feel free to reach out. I'm here to help in any way I can." There's a scoff from behind me, and my cheeks flame.

The sound of people packing up fills my ears, and I take my time in cleaning off the whiteboard I'd scribbled all over during the lesson and restacking some of the text books on the shelves beneath that were a little untidy.

A few 'thank yous' and 'see you next weeks' ring out, and I acknowledge each one with a hesitant glance towards the student.

I don't turn back around until I'm confident everyone has gone, and even then it's only to grab my bag so I can get away from here and all the thoughts he conjures up in my head.

"Shit. Fuck." My hand comes up to cover my racing heart when I find him still sitting at his desk with his feet once again on the fucking top and his chair rocking back. A surefire way to piss off any teacher.

"Did you need help with the assignment, Mr. Kingsman?"

"Um...no, I think I've got it covered." His feet hit the floor and he stands, taking all the air in the room with him as he stalks towards me.

My heart continues to race and my palms start to sweat as he approaches the other side of the desk.

"I was more wondering what I could do for you."

"How's that?" I squeak. Wishing the ground would swallow me up for showing my vulnerability, I reach for my pencil case, ready to stuff it inside my bag, but he stops me. His large, calloused hand lands on mine, and I'm forced to freeze as sparks shoot up my arm. I glance at the door, knowing that Eddie will most probably barge through at any moment to check up on me.

"I'm not totally sure. I was hoping you could help me out with that."

When I turn back to him, he's staring at me

with narrowed eyes as if he's trying to work me out. My lips part to respond, but he beats me to it.

"What I do know is that what you need isn't Mr. Boring, and it also isn't this poncy fucking twinset." He reaches out and pops open the top button of my cardigan like a freaking magic trick. "I also know that you're looking for something, and I'm pretty sure I can help you find it."

"I uh..." I've no idea what to say to any of that other than to be freaked out by how spot-on his assumptions are.

"You don't need to tell me that I'm right. I already have my answer." His smug smirk pisses me off, but it's nowhere near enough for me to make him leave. "So, are you in?"

"In with what exactly?" My eyes find the door again as I try to pull my hand from under his, not wanting to get caught in this position, but he squeezes harder to stop me.

"Giving me a chance to find whatever it is you're looking for."

"I've no idea what—" The door opens. My eyes fly up and my heart pounds against my ribs as Joe rips his hand from mine and steps back.

"You all done for the—Mr. Kingsman, in

trouble again?" Eddie looks between the two of us, his eyes calculating.

"Not this time. Just had a couple of important questions for Miss Smith before I left to make a start on my assignment in the coffee shop down the street." He turns back to me and winks.

It's probably the most unsubtle invitation I've ever heard. I expect Eddie to say something but, to my surprise, he side-steps Joe's random statement. "You ready?"

I hesitate for a second, giving Joe a chance to return to his seat and pick up his bag, but he's not yet out of the room when I say, "Actually, I'll find my own way home tonight. I've got a few errands to run. I wouldn't want to hold you up."

"Oh, okay. If you're sure."

I barely hear the words, because I'm too focused on the wide, triumphant smile Joe graces me with before he walks out of my classroom.

What the hell are you doing, Quinn?

I tell myself that I'm just going to get a coffee for the journey home. I want to see if he's really there and what else he has to say. I'd be lying if I said I wasn't interested in hearing it.

I feel him watching me the second I step inside the coffee shop, but I come up empty when I quickly scan the tables as I walk towards the counter.

"Cappuccino, one sugar, chocolate sprinkles," is whispered in my ear, sending goosebumps racing across my skin.

Turning, I find him right behind me with two mugs in hand.

"How'd you know?"

"Good guess."

I follow him to a table in a dark corner at the back of the shop, my entire body shaking with nervous energy, and sit with my hands wrapped around the mug so he doesn't see them trembling.

"So tell me, Miss Smith. What is it you're looking for?"

"I don't—'

"Don't lie to me. I can see it in your eyes every time you look at me. Tell me what you need. I'm sure I can deliver everything you desire."

Need sits heavy in my stomach. I might be wanting to experience new things, but there's no way in hell I'm asking him to cure that little issue.

"I want..." I hesitate, and he leans forward as if I'm about to tell him a secret. "To really live. To do all the things I've never been able to do." A rush of adrenaline hits me at admitting that out loud for the first time in my life.

I expect him to laugh, because it's more than obvious that this guy does exactly what he wants and when he wants, but all he does is rest his arms on the table and ask, "Like what?"

"So many things. I want to wear the clothes I want, I want to dance to the music I want, I want to get drunk and dance all night, get a tattoo, have a one nig—" I stop when his eyes widen in delight. That's not what this is about.

A man clears his throat behind Joe, and I damn near jump out of the chair thinking that we've been caught, but when I look up there's just a man helping his wife into her coat.

"Why haven't you done any of this before?" he asks, ignoring my skittishness, sipping on his own coffee and swallowing his reaction to what I almost admitted.

"I lived a somewhat sheltered life."

"In London?"

I shake my head, already knowing that I've revealed too much. "I've only just moved here."

"So I was right earlier about the twinset, then." His eyes drop to my chest, and I sigh.

"I fucking hate them."

"Right." He tips his mug up to finish off what's left and stands. "Let's go, then."

"Where?" I ask, my eyes wide in shock.

"To experience life."

"Uh..."

"What, you scared?"

"No, I..." His eyebrow lifts in challenge, but there's no way I'm backing down. "Just need to finish my coffee first."

"Oh...wild," he says with a laugh, sitting himself back down.

CHAPTER FIVE

JOE WAITS around the corner as I run back into the college and drop my bags off in the staff room. Thankfully, the department is empty, and I don't run into any colleagues who've only just seen me leave.

I don't allow myself time to think about the reality of what I've just agreed to. Instead, I focus on the excitement of what he might be about to show me.

I find him in a hidden doorway on his phone when I get back outside.

"I thought maybe you were going to bail."

"I don't back down from a challenge, Mr. Kingsman."

"Joe, please. I can't cope with all this surname bollocks."

"Sure thing. Where first?"

"To get rid of that godawful twinset."

"Won't all the shops be shut?"

"You really haven't been here long, huh?" I shake my head in response and fall into step beside him. "This is London. You can get anything whenever you want it."

"I don't have much money," I admit with a wince.

"Okay, we'll steer clear of Bond Street then." He chuckles. "I'm not sure they'll have the kind of thing we're after, anyway."

Side by side, we walk towards the tube station. He looks relaxed as ever while I feel like I could pass out any minute at the rate my heart's pounding in my chest. I might be breaking all the rules, but I'm about to get a taste of the life I've always wanted, I'm sure of it.

"I've never stepped foot inside a Topshop before."

"Where did you come from? Narnia?"

"Might as well have been," I mutter as we descend the escalator.

"We'll need to be quick. They close soon."

We step from the escalator and Joe darts right, as if he knows exactly where he's going.

"Do you trust me?"

"Uh..."

"Go to the fitting rooms, get undressed, and I'll get some options."

"How much do you know about women's clothes?"

"Enough. Now go."

Thankfully, there's no assistant hovering at the fitting rooms, so I rush into the first cubicle and strip out of my twinset.

Standing there in my boring cotton underwear, I start to question my sanity. I'm standing basically naked waiting for one of my students to bring me a new outfit to wear on a crazy night out.

I should be concerned, but everything I've been worrying about seems to vanish when I'm with him. That might freak me out, but it's also such a relief after looking over my shoulder every second since I arrived here.

"Quinn?"

"In here." I poke my head out of the curtain. Joe's eyes drop despite the fact that I've got the curtain draped around me.

"Put these on." He thrusts a couple of hangers at me, and I slink back behind the curtain.

"Uh...where's the rest of the top?" I ask, eyeing the tiny bit of fabric in my hands.

"Probably in the bin, which is exactly where that bloody twinset is going in a few minutes. Now stop complaining and put it on."

Rolling my eyes at him, I pull the skinny black jeans from the hanger and attempt to pull them up my legs. I feel like Sandy as she tried to get those leather trousers on in *Grease*.

Amazingly, they fit like a second skin, and even I can appreciate how good they look. I've never seen my legs like this before. I always thought I was a little short and stumpy, but I'm realising that might have been the a-line skirts.

Next, I remove the scrap of fabric that I'm assuming is meant to be a top from the hanger and pull it on. What little there is of it is covered in silver sequins. It's short enough to expose my midriff, something I can honestly say has never seen the light of day before, and apart from the spaghetti straps across the back, it totally exposes that as well.

"I'm not sure about this," I say to the curtain.

"Show me," he demands.

"Fuck." I stare at myself in the mirror, and it's like there's a different woman looking back at me. Gone is the boring, nondescript woman I'm used to, and in her place is a stylish, young lady who has the city at her feet.

I run my fingers through my bobbed hair in an attempt to give it some volume and blow out a deep breath.

My hand shakes as I lift it to pull the curtain back. The second it's in my hand, I shut my eyes and just go for it.

"Fuuuuuck," Joe groans, and my eyes pop open in horror. Only, the expression on his face doesn't show that of disapproval like I was expecting. It's full of heat, and the sight of it has desire pooling between my legs.

"I feel naked," I admit, covering my bare stomach with my hands.

"Trust me, you're anything but naked right now."

"I've never shown this much skin," I whisper, more to myself than him. I know it's crazy, seeing as I'm wearing a full-length pair of jeans, but still. It's the top that makes me feel so exposed.

Lifting his arm, he signals for me to spin around for him.

Sucking in as much confidence as I can muster, I close my eyes and begin turning.

"Waaaait."

"What?" I look over my shoulder when his warmth hits my bare skin.

"This," he says, snapping my bra strap, "needs to go."

"I don't think so."

"Trust me." Before I even have time to consider if I do or not, the fabric around my ribs loosens and he's pulling the straps down my arms.

"What the hell are you doing?"

"Pushing you out of your comfort zone and making you live."

"Why the hell did I admit that to you?" I mutter, taking over the job of removing my bra. The second I pull it out from under the tiny sequined top, I really feel naked. The fabric tickles against the sensitive skin of my breasts, and the cool air surrounds them. My nipples pucker, but thankfully the sequins cover it. Showing him just how much this is affecting me is the last thing I want.

"Because you know I'm the one to do it. And if it was a one-night-stand you were too scared to admit to wanting, you shouldn't have any problems looking like you do right now." One of his hands brushes up my exposed spine, and his breath tickles across my neck.

I shudder, and there's no way in hell he doesn't notice.

"What the hell?"

He steps back, giving me a little space to breathe, but then he pulls the back of the jeans away from me and tugs at the tag. "Do you have any regard for people's personal space?"

He rolls his eyes and reaches out again, I assume for the tag on the top, but knowing it's currently pressed against my right breast, I turn away from him and pull it off myself.

"You planning on ruining all my fun?"

"You ask that like you're not having the time of your life right now."

The smile that curls at his lips makes my breath catch.

"What size feet are you?"

"Five, why?"

He glances down at the cute ballet shoes I wore to work today and quirks an eyebrow.

"Fine. But I'm keeping them. I only bought them a few days ago."

"Fine. Sort your shit out, and I'll meet you at the entrance."

He takes off with the clothing tags, and I panic. "You're not paying for those." He doesn't bother to turn around and respond. Instead, he lifts his hand over his shoulder and flips me off.

I fume, my fists clenching. Why did the guy who caught my eye have to be so infuriating?

I fold all my old clothes into a shopping bag that's at the bottom of my handbag and slip my feet into my comfortable flats. I dread to think what he's going to find for me.

When I emerge, the shop is deserted. I start to panic that I've been locked in until I take a few more steps and find my partner in crime standing to the side of the doors with a pair of black strappy sandals swinging from his fingers and a woman's leather jacket draped over his arm.

"There's no way I can walk in those."

As if he knows just how competitive I am, he drops his gaze to my feet before he says, "I bet you can. Loser buys dinner."

"Jesus," I mutter, holding my hand out.

He offers his support once I've got the first shoe on my foot and start wobbling about as I attempt the second one. The moment his fingers wrap around mine, sparks fly up my arm. My eyes search his out, and, when I find them, he's staring right back at me.

"I don't want a one-night-stand," I blurt out, probably sounding like a total moron.

"That's good, because I wasn't offering one."

"Really?"

My eyes search his. From the way he was looking at me earlier and the way he touched me, I was convinced that was where he hoped this was heading.

"I'm not the type of man to do that kind of thing." He reaches out and tucks a lock of my hair behind my ear. The move is so soft and gentle, the total opposite to what I'd expect from looking at him.

"I don't believe that for a second. I saw you—" I cut myself off when I realise I'm about to admit to watching him the other night.

"You saw me what? Have you been stalking me, Miss Smith?"

"What? No. It's just...Eddie took me to The Avenue last week and you were...enjoying yourself."

"Ah, I see," he says sadly. Dropping my hand, he turns to leave.

"Wait." Without thinking, I slide my hand back into his when I catch up with him. "You just looked like you were having fun. I was...jealous."

"Jealous? Wasn't Mr. Boring keeping you entertained?"

"He took me to the VIP section. It's not really my kind of thing. I'd have been much happier down with you."

"That's because I'm such a good dancer."

"I saw. Everyone seemed to love you."

"I know how to show them a good time."

"So what are you waiting for? I want a good time."

CHAPTER SIX

———

OUR FIRST STOP isn't the craziest of locations. I was kind of hoping he'd dive right in with the wild night he had planned. That said, takeout Chinese sitting in the middle of Leicester Square is pretty awesome.

"Oh my god, this is so good," I moan around a mouthful of sticky chicken. Aside from going out for dinner with Eddie, my diet has been pretty limited since I moved here, so this tastes incredible. "You've got to try some. Here." I hold out my fork for him, and, after a slight hesitation, he opens his mouth. I realise my mistake almost immediately. His full lips wrap around my fork, and I can't take my eyes away from them as he chews and then swipes his tongue across the bottom one to lick up some stray sauce.

"Keep looking at me like that and I'll get the wrong idea about what you want from me tonight."

His words cause desire to fill my veins, but as much as I'm enjoying his company, I know I can't allow anything to happen. He's my student. What I'm doing with him now is forbidden, let alone if I was to take it any further.

"So how come you've gone back to school?" I ask, trying to steer our conversation back to safe ground.

"I fucked it up first time around. Believe it or not, I was a bit of a nightmare teenager."

"I don't believe that for a second," I say with a laugh. He's got the bad boy image now—I can only imagine what he was like as a kid.

"I didn't care back then. My only focus was pissing my parents off as much as possible. But now, I want more."

"Good for you. There are so many people who just put up with what life dealt them. Not everyone has the guts to admit they might have screwed up and do something to better themselves."

"I've got balls, don't you worry about that." He

winks, and I can't help but laugh. This guy does something to me, something I've never experienced before, but the world seems that little bit better when he's by my side. It's crazy. Unbelievable. But true.

"So what's the plan then?"

"Oh god, you're one of those, aren't you?"

"One of those?" My brows draw together as I wait for him to explain.

"Control freak. I've got a couple of friends like you."

"Guilty."

"Well, switch it off. Tonight, you follow my lead and do as you're told."

"Okay, lead the way."

He takes us back to the tube, thankfully, remembering the slow pace I need with these damn shoes on. I guess I could take them off now I won the bet and he had to pay for dinner, but I quite like them. They give me confidence that I'm not used to by standing a little taller, and that's something I need seeing as I'm walking around practically topless.

He takes me to a comedy club on the outskirts of Camden Town and, unlike Eddie, when he goes to the bar he orders us two pints.

I know it's not really anything in the grand scheme of things, but sitting there drinking a pint when a lady doing such a thing was so frowned upon where I came from, I feel like I can take on the world.

"What are you smiling at?" Joe asks when there's a break in comedians.

"Nothing. Everything."

"Okay. Care to explain?"

Shaking my head, I take another sip of my beer. "I just really needed this."

"Yeah, me too." He lifts his drink and takes a sip. He winks at me over the rim, telling me that he knows he's giving me an out from having to explain anything.

I've opened up more to him than I have anyone ever—and that's saying something, because he doesn't really know anything. Eddie knows the most about my life, but that's only because he experienced some of it first hand, one thing I never forget every time he looks at me.

The next comedian up on stage is a woman, and after only two minutes I've got tears streaming down my face. She's by far the funniest person I've ever heard, and the more I laugh the more I forget about the skeletons in my closet and just enjoy my new life.

"You're beautiful when you smile," Joe says, leaning over and whispering in my ear.

I'd felt him staring at me as I laughed at her dry, witty jokes, but I wasn't able to pull my eyes away.

"Even with the tears?"

"Even with them, babe."

"Uh..." Warmth spreads through my body, desire that I'd managed to dampen down erupting as I turn and take in his soft eyes and smile.

"Ready to move on?"

Hand in hand, we walk towards the centre of Camden Town. Joe drags me into the first place that has music pounding out of the doors.

"Drink?" he asks, although I can barely hear him over the live music coming from the stage at the other end of the bar.

"Um..." I grab the menu, but it's plucked from my hand.

"I'll choose. Go grab that seat." Unlike when Eddie ordered for me, frustration doesn't bubble up within me. Weirdly, I trust Joe to get something I'm going to like, not just something he thinks will impress me.

I hover as the couple vacating the table leave, grateful not to have to stand up in these shoes for much longer.

"What's this?" I take a sip of the drink.

"Slippery nipple."

"I'm sorry, what?" I almost spray him with the creamy liquid.

"It's a cocktail called a slippery nipple. You made out earlier that you'd lived a sheltered life, so I assumed you'd not had one before. The drink, I mean," he adds when my cheeks flame.

Why is it that the second he says that, the only thing I can see is him sucking my—no. Totally inappropriate.

As if he knows exactly where my head's at, his eyes drop to my chest. "Although, I could certainly arrange for the other kind, if you fancy it."

A bolt of lust hits me so hard I think I'd be on the floor if I wasn't already sitting. My lips part as my breathing increases. A wicked smile twitches at his lips as his eyes bounce between mine and my lips. I really should do something to stop this. My thoughts vanish when he reaches across the table and tangles our fingers together.

Thankfully, the music starts again, cutting off any more inappropriate comments that might be on the tip of his tongue. I can tell by the darkness of his eyes and the twitching muscle in his neck that he's thinking of plenty.

Turning my focus away from him, I look at the band up on stage and try to ignore the need sitting heavy in my stomach. He, however, doesn't turn away from me throughout their entire set.

Needing a little space to breathe, I excuse myself to the bathroom. The music is still loud as I do my business, but even though I wanted some space, the second I'm away from him, I find myself looking over my shoulder once again before rushing back to the safety of his side.

I find two fresh drinks waiting for me at the table when I retake my seat.

"Should I ask?"

He chuckles as he goes back to the bar to grab his beer, but instead of taking his seat, he comes up behind me and whispers, "The clear one with the olive is a martini—dirty, of course. And the other, that's something else I think you might be in need of."

"Oh?"

"A screaming orgasm." My breath catches as his nose—or lips, I'm not really sure—runs around the shell of my ear. My wanton moan only serves to prove to both of us that that could possibly be exactly what I need.

It doesn't mean you're going to allow it to happen, a little voice screams inside my head. I just about manage to hear her over the blood racing in my ears as I wonder just how good he'd be at giving me a real one of those and not just the cocktail.

He's gone as fast as he appeared, and by the time I look up he's sitting in his seat, sipping on his beer like those few seconds didn't happen.

"What?" he asks when he places his glass down and finds me staring at him with my mouth still agape.

"N-nothing."

"Good, drink up. I've got plans."

"More?"

"Didn't you tell me that you wanted to stay up all night and experience London?"

"I guess."

"Well, what kind of friend would I be if I didn't make that happen?"

Friend. *Friend.* The word feels wrong, but the reality is that even being friends is against the rules. And I know for a fact that wanting more, like what he just whispered in my ear, would smash all the rules to smithereens.

CHAPTER SEVEN

I HAVE no clue what the time is, and quite frankly I don't care. That could be due to the amount of alcohol I've put away tonight, or it could be the company, I've no idea. But as we dance together in the basement of a club that I can't for the life of me remember the name of, I realise that I feel more alive than I have done in…forever. And it's not just this place that does that, it's him. He makes me feel like the woman I've always wanted to be. He makes me feel whole, and I've only just met him.

"Stop thinking," he whispers in my ear, his hands finding my hips and pulling me back into his body.

He's been fairly well behaved since he whispered naughty things about screaming orgasms in my ear at the bar. I must admit that I expected him to pull me to him the moment he dragged me onto the dancefloor. I'd witnessed him dancing before, and I'd be lying if I said I didn't want to experience what it would be like to move my hips in time with his like the girls that night.

"Sorry, just trying to process everything."

"Well, stop. The only thing you should be doing right now is feeling. Feel the music. Feel your body moving in time to the beat, and feel the tension that's pulling your shoulders tight wash away."

"O-okay," I stutter as his groin rolls against my arse. A tremble races through me, and my body follows his lead.

"Better," he whispers when I relax against him. "Just go with the flow."

Something about those words make me tense again. I've gone with the flow my entire life—that's how I ended up stuck where I was. But I soon realise that this is different. Joe's version of going with the flow doesn't involve some of the things my previous life did. His version is about letting go and having fun. Exactly what I told him I wanted.

His fingers dig into my hips a little more,

forcing me to shut down my thoughts and just move.

I press back into him, our bodies lining up perfectly. His movements are perfectly in sync with the music. The bass pounds so loud that the floor beneath me vibrates, and it only adds to the tingles that are already surging around my body at being so close to him.

Resting my head back against his shoulder, my eyes fall shut and I soak up the moment. There's every possibility that I might not get this chance again. I could be found and dragged back to face the music at any moment. It's a fact that I can never forget as I constantly look over my shoulder, waiting for an unwanted familiar face.

I've no idea how much time passes or how many songs play while we stand in the exact same position, moving against each other. My aching feet seem to vanish along with the hundreds of people around us. The only thing I notice is that the more I rub my arse against Joe, the harder his cock presses into me. The knowledge that I'm the one doing that fills me with so much delight I can barely wipe the smile off my face. I'm not sure I've ever really turned anyone on before. I can say with absolute certainty that I've never experienced the tension that's sizzling between us right now.

My pulse thunders through my veins and the unmistakable throb between my legs intensifies. I've no doubt the man behind me could help me experience things I've been missing out on, but as incredible as this feels right now, I still can't forget the reasons why it shouldn't be happening.

A growl rumbles up his throat before his breath tickles my ear. "If I didn't know better, I'd think you were doing that on purpose. I didn't think you wanted that tonight, Miss Smith."

I have no words, so when I open my mouth, the only thing that comes out is a needy moan.

"Jesus. You have any idea how badly I need you right now?" My chest heaves as excitement explodes in my belly.

Those few words should be enough to make me step away, to put the space between us that there should be, but in reality, they do the opposite. With his scent surrounding me and the effects of the alcohol controlling my body, I want everything he has to offer.

"Joe," I moan, turning my head so my nose runs along the skin of his neck. I breathe in his woodsy scent, and it only makes my need for him stronger.

He looks down at me. The moment our eyes connect, I think he's going to take everything he wants, and a slither of terror runs through me.

But he doesn't.

He doesn't drop his head. His lips don't find mine. His hand, however...that does move. The rough skin of his palm scratches up the smooth skin of my stomach until his fingers slip inside the fabric of my top.

He reaches my ribs, and I swear I stop breathing. My breasts swell with the need to be touched, my nipples pebble against the heavy fabric hanging over them, and heat floods my core in anticipation.

Time stands still as his hand continues to move. The second his thumb brushes against the underside of my breast, I suck in a huge breath.

"Oh god," I moan, pressing back harder into him as I almost lose the use of my legs.

His hand cups my breast, and I swear I nearly fall apart from that alone. He pinches my nipple between his thumb and forefinger, and my eyes flutter shut so I can focus on the sensation racing through my body.

My chest heaves, my heart races, and my head

spins. He's barely touching me, but I'm falling apart at the seams.

"You think I can give you that screaming orgasm from this alone?"

My response is a whimper.

His hips keep moving against my arse, his cock now impossibly hard against me. My core clenches with need to feel him inside me.

"I bet you taste so sweet. If we were anywhere else, I'd rip that fabric from your body and find out. Would you want that?"

Whimper.

He palms my breast again. Even the mention of where we are right now doesn't concern me. I'm too lost to him and the sensations he's erupting in my body.

"I'd lick and suck until you were begging for more." His voice is barely a whisper, but the deep, rumbling timbre has heat blooming low in my stomach.

His other hand teases at the waistband of my jeans.

"You think anyone would notice if I were to find out how wet you are for me right now?"

Whimper.

"Are you ready for me, Miss Smith?" He

pinches each nipple harder, pulling them harshly, the action sending lightning bolts to my core. A ball of something explosive grows within me to the point that I feel like I'm about to break apart. My temperature spikes, my heart pounds, and then it happens. Lights flash behind my eyes, and something explodes within me. Wave after wave of pleasure so intense hits me again and again, threatening to buckle my knees.

"Holy fuck." His deep, gravelly voice has aftershocks shooting off around my body.

Dropping his hand from my top, he spins me in his arms. I keep my eyes locked on his shoulder as his arms wrap around my waist. I'm too embarrassed by what just happened to risk looking up into his eyes.

If he says anything, I don't hear it, but his fingers press under my chin and I'm powerless but to allow him to tip my head back.

The desire in his eyes has my breath catching in my throat. His tongue sneaks out and captures my attention as it runs along his bottom lip. My mouth waters as he leans in. I expect his lips to press to mine, but he surprises me once again when he moves to whisper in my ear. "I'm pretty sure that was the hottest thing I've ever experienced."

He's clearly got a lot more experience in this stuff than me, so I highly doubt his words are true. If he had the balls to do what he just did to me while surrounded by hundreds of people, then I've no doubt he's done much, much worse. The thought has disappointment cooling the fire that's still burning within me.

I know for a fact that it's the hottest thing *I've* ever experienced. I'm not a virgin by any means, but when I think back to my previous encounters, the term 'lie back and think of England' comes to mind.

My cheeks heat as I think about my first orgasm being delivered in the middle of a night club.

"You're beautiful when you blush." Unable to hold his eyes, I look over his shoulder. The sincerity pouring from them is a little much to take. "You want to get out of here?"

"Sure." *I think that's probably for the best.* Somehow, I manage to keep that last thought to myself.

Joe threads his fingers through mine and, after stopping to collect our coats and my bags, we head out into the night.

"What time is it?"

"Almost four."

"Four in the morning?" I ask, disbelief filling my voice.

"Yeah. How do you feel, having almost done your full all-nighter?"

"Weirdly not tired."

"Good, because we haven't finished yet."

"No?"

"No. You might want to change your shoes, though. We're going for a night time tour of the city."

The moment he mentions my shoes, all feeling comes back to my feet, and they throb.

Joe holds onto my elbow as I pull the sandals off and slip on my much more comfortable flats. Then we set off.

I've no idea if he has a destination in mind, but I don't really care. I'd follow him to the end of the earth right now if it meant I continued feeling the way I am.

Not once do I look over my shoulder to see if we're being followed, and not a second passes in which I think about my past. It's exactly where it belongs when I'm with Joe: in the past.

By the time he pulls me into a twenty-four hour shop and off licence, we've walked miles and the alcohol that was running through my system has long since disappeared—that is, until he purchases a bottle of tequila.

"You're joking, right? We're not drinking that now?"

"Hair of the dog. It'll help set you up for the day."

The thought of a full day at work has realisation setting in. "Fuck."

"Exactly. But I've got plenty of experience when it comes to partying all night. So are you with me?" He twists the top off the second we emerge from the electric lights of the small shop and takes a swig. He winces as it burns but happily hands it over.

"To going crazy and pulling all nighters," I say with a laugh and lift it to my lips. "Ugh," I complain once I've swallowed it, discovering that there's a reason I've never had this before.

"To unexpected all nighters with beautiful strangers."

When he offers me the bottle again, I stupidly take another shot. It almost immediately makes my head spin.

"Right, we need breakfast to soak this up."

"So we're not going home to bed, then?"

He turns his heated stare on me and I instantly regret the question. "There would only be one reason we'd end up in bed tonight, babe, and it wouldn't be for sleeping." My lips form an O, my heart pounding rapidly. If he could get me off as easily as he did in the club when we were both fully dressed, I can only imagine how skilled he might be once naked. "But you said no one-night-stand, so breakfast it is."

With the half-empty bottle of tequila in one hand and mine in the other, we set off once again.

He directs us to a kebab shop and takes the liberty of ordering for both of us. I'm grateful, because I'd have no clue what to order anyway. I'm a kebab virgin, although I'm not drunk enough to admit that one out loud.

CHAPTER EIGHT

JOE DROPS me off at my building just before sunrise with a sweet kiss on the cheek and a sexy smile.

He was the perfect gentleman, aside from those few moments in the club, and as I climb the stairs to my tiny flat, I can't wipe the smile off my face. Who knew that bad boy who turned up to his first lesson looking so unsure of himself would help me cross a few things off my to do list with such style?

"Shit," I gasp when I see the clock on the oven as I let myself in. I've only got an hour until I need to teach my first class of the day.

I peel my new clothes from my body and step into my shower, needing to wash the scent of last night's alcohol and nightclub from my body. If I'm intending to go to work still slightly intoxicated, at least I can make an effort to smell fresh.

Seeing as I've still not been to the bloody laundrette, I'm stuck with the only thing left in my wardrobe: a baby pink twinset and a grey a-line skirt. I can't help laughing as I pull it on, thinking about what Joe's opinion would be. He'd probably want to rip it from my body if he were to catch me wearing it. Those thoughts have memories of his hands on me last night consuming me as I blow dry my hair and apply my makeup.

I stop off and pick up a large cappuccino with a double shot of coffee in the coffee shop where everything started last night. I can't help wishing that we could do it all over again. It was by far the best night of my life and totally worth the exhaustion that's starting to take over my body right about now.

MY FIRST CLASS of the day has just settled into its first task when my phone vibrates against my desk. Risking a glance at it, my lips twitch into a smile when I see his ridiculous email address.

To: *Quinn Smith*
From: *Tatstwatsandarseholes*
Subject: *I can show you the world...*

Dear Miss Smith
I hope you enjoyed your magic carpet ride and
aren't feeling the effects too badly this morning.
If you ask me, it could easily be turned into an epic
love story.
I'm ready to analyse the next chapter if you are.
Yours,
Mr. Kingsman

My phone trembles in my hand. I shouldn't be doing this, and I really shouldn't be this excited about it.

I'm still staring at it when a shadow falls over me. "Shit," I squeak, shoving my phone deep into my bag when I find Eddie at the other side of my desk, also looking down at my phone.

"Morning," I sing happily, hoping to cover up the blush on my cheeks and the fact I only drank some tequila a couple of hours ago.

"Is...everything okay?" His brows are drawn together as he assesses me.

"Y-yeah, of course. This class is great."

"I was asking about you. You look like you didn't get any sleep last night." My heart immediately thunders against my chest. Fuck, does he know?

My hands tremble as he continues to stare at me.

"I've...uh...just got a lot on my mind."

"Everything's okay though, with all that? You'd tell me if you needed something, right?"

"Of course. Everything's fine. I've not heard anything."

My words must be sincere enough, because after a couple of seconds Eddie nods and turns to leave.

I push my bag under my desk and attempt to ignore my phone's existence.

Trying to think about anything but him as well as keeping myself awake, I do a lap of my classroom and check in on each student. This class is a little more of what I'm used to, seeing as the majority are still teenagers. That being said, they're still a million miles from the private school kids of my past.

"How are you doing, Jodi?" I ask, dropping down to my haunches and checking on one of the quieter members of the group. There's something so familiar about her. She reminds me of a younger me. There's a sadness in her eyes that only comes with the overbearing nature of my past.

"I'm good, Miss, thank you." Her words are as quiet as a mouse.

"You can call me Quinn, sweetie. If you need anything, please just ask. I'm here to help." I can't help but offer my support, although I'm sure how much I really mean it goes straight over her head.

Thoughts of my past along with memories of last night fill my mind for the rest of the morning.

I grab myself a panini from the coffee shop around the corner for lunch, and by the time my belly is full it's all I can do to keep my eyes open in the quiet of our little staff room. Pushing my diary and laptop aside, I lay my head on my arms just for a few moments to relax.

I awake to the sound of someone clearing their throat.

Lifting my head, I instantly meet the concerned eyes of Eddie, who's down on his haunches looking at me.

"Are you sure you're okay?"

"I promise." I smile weakly, my sleep-fogged brain making any kind of movement hard right now.

"If I didn't know any better, I'd think you went out last night. Have you made some new friends?"

"No," I lie smoothly. "I had a glass of wine too many with dinner," I admit, realising that he's close enough to possibly smell last night on me.

"Be sensible. I know life's different for you now, but please don't go too wild."

He eyes me as I panic. My palms sweat as I think about what could possibly happen to me if he were to find out what I did last night and with whom.

"I won't. I just needed a little help to relax." It's not a lie. It's exactly what last night was.

"Just remember, I'm here for you."

"I know. Thank you."

The second he leaves the room, my head finds the desk again—only this time it's not to sleep, it's out of frustration for what I'm doing.

The last thing I needed when I stepped out of the building to finally head home later that afternoon was an almighty downpour.

I watch as Londoners run past the front doors to the college building, using anything they've got in their hands to protect themselves from the torrential water. A couple of people shelter in the doorway, but I don't have time for this. My need to be at home and in my pyjamas tops my need to stay dry right now.

A shiver runs down my spine as the cold hits me, but it still doesn't deter me. A warm shower will fix everything.

I'm rushing towards the tube station when a white van comes to a screeching halt right in front of me.

I freeze in terror. My heart races and my head spins as memories hit me.

I can't go back.

My chest heaves as I try to drag in some much-needed oxygen and pull myself together. If they've come for me, I need to prepare for what happens next.

I'm busy mentally building the walls back up that had started to crumble last night when the passenger window opens.

"You fucking getting in or not?"

It takes me a couple of seconds to figure out who it is. The voice is so familiar, and the deep timbre to it has tingles erupting within me, but the sight is anything but what I'm used to.

He's dirty—disgusting actually—but he's never looked better.

My muscles still refuse to move as I stare at his

messy hair flopping down onto his forehead, the dark smears covering his face from a long, hard day at work, and the dirty, ripped white t-shirt stretched across this wide chest.

I'm in trouble.

"Do I need to come and put you inside myself?" Although the prospect of that happening has fire racing through my veins, I manage to force my legs to work and take a step towards him.

"No, it's okay," I whisper, but with the sound of the rain hitting the pavement and the hustle and bustle of London in the background, there's no way he hears me.

"Hey," he says when I drop down onto his passenger seat and wipe the rain from my face.

"Hey." I risk a look up at him, and my breath catches in my throat. "Whoa," I breathe. If I thought he looked good from a distance, it's nothing compared to him close-up with his scent filling my nose.

"What?" he asks with a chuckle. "Dirty workmen your thing?"

"Apparently so." The words aren't meant to be said aloud, but it's too late now. His eyes darken and drop down to my lips for a beat. My cheeks heat and my thighs clench.

"And here I was thinking women wanted knights in shining armour."

"Nah, a dirty guy in a work van is good for me." I slam my lips shut, praying that I can put an end to the things that seem to be falling from my mouth.

Glancing at him out of the corner of my eye as I buckle up, I find a sexy smirk playing on his lips. Damn him for knowing how sexy he is.

My eyes slowly travel up his exposed arm, taking in all his ink and wondering what the story behind each one is as he pulls away and back into the Friday night rush hour traffic.

"How are you feeling?" he asks, focusing on where he's going and ignoring my attention.

Hot. "I'm okay. I had a little cat nap in the office this afternoon. You?"

"Much better now I've seen you."

I chuckle. "You always this smooth?"

"Always," he confirms. "So no nightmare students to deal with today?"

"Nope. I've only got one. He's in my Thursday night class. Sits at the back with a smirk on his face and feet up on the desk like he owns the place."

"Sounds like a nightmare."

"You've no idea. He drives me crazy."

I don't need to look over to know that he's

smiling. I can feel the amusement coming off him in waves. It's almost as strong as the desire coursing through my veins.

Silence fills the small cab of his van until the tension and crackling chemistry between us almost hits breaking point.

I really need to stay away from this man.

"So...was last night everything you hoped it would be?"

I want to tell him that it was that and so much more, but I also don't want him to know just how much it meant to me. I've already shown too much of myself to him. "Yeah, it was good."

"Good?"

"Yeah, it was fun."

"Fun. Huh?"

"What's that meant to mean?"

"Nothing. Just wondering what I should have done to make it amazing."

I pause, because I think we both know that it was amazing, even if I'm too scared to admit it. "Well...it didn't tick off all my crazy to-do list."

"No one-night-stand. Right."

"That wasn't on my list," I protest.

"Sure."

"How was your day at work?" I ask, trying to steer the conversation away from me.

"Long. Boring. Everything that last night wasn't. Plus, you weren't there."

Looking over, my eyes find his staring back at me, and my breath catches. The sincerity in his stare is a little much to take. I'm not sure anyone's ever looked at me with such honesty and longing in their eyes.

"I don't think I should have got in this van with you."

"Why?"

"Shit," I mutter. The more I try to be unaffected by him, the more he buries his way under my skin.

He turns back to watch where we're going, but I can't rip my eyes away from his profile. His jaw is covered in the perfect amount of scruff, and his full lips are parted slightly, allowing his breaths to pass. His neck and shoulders are pure muscle, and his chest is rising and falling rapidly, showing me that although he seems calm and composed by this situation, in reality it's hitting him just like it is me.

He turns back towards me, his eyes like blue pools of desire that I really shouldn't want to dip my toe into, I'm afraid I might not be able to stop myself. He holds my stare once again, allowing me to see exactly what it is he wants. Memories from the club last night hit me, and I feel it right in my core. What it felt like to have his hands on me. How he so easily played my body until I totally fell apart in his arms.

"You don't need to be afraid to ask me for what you need."

I suck in a surprised breath. Did I just say something aloud again?

His hand lifts from his lap, and the rough skin brushes across my cheek, sending shudders of pleasure through my body.

Ripping my eyes away from his, I take in my surroundings. My building.

My heart drops that our time is over, until I see the movement of a shadow over by the bushes.

The fear that consumed me when Joe's van pulled up in front of me is strong enough to overtake my desire. My eyes dart around, looking for anything else out of place, and it doesn't go unnoticed.

"Are you okay?"

"I...uh...of course. Thank you for the lift." I squash the tremble in my voice, but the concern that twists his face tells me I didn't do a very good job.

My hand shakes as adrenaline races through my limbs when I reach for the door.

"Would you like me to walk you up?"

I should say no. I'm well aware of that. But I'm also aware that if I were to come face-to-face with my past, having Joe standing behind me would be no bad thing. Not that I have any intention of dragging him into my disastrous past life.

"N-no, I'll be fine." My voice cracks, and I hate sounding so weak and vulnerable.

Pushing the door open, I climb out into the rain. A shiver runs through me as the cold surrounds me. I look back for Joe, regretting my decision, but when I look into the van, it's empty.

My brows pull together, but only for a second because the warmth of his arm wrapping around my waist gives me a clue as to where he is.

"Come on. Let's get out of the rain."

The beep of his van locking sounds out behind us as he guides me towards the building. I make quick work of letting us in, and he silently follows me up the stairs to my door.

I come to a stop with my key in my hand, ready to let myself inside, but I don't get to push it into the lock because Joe reaches out and wraps his fingers around mine.

My eyes focus on his cotton covered chest for a few seconds as I try to muster up the strength I'm going to need to look into his eyes. When I do lift my head, I realise that no amount of time could have prepared me for the heated gaze staring back at me.

My mouth waters. I swallow it down as I try to come up with the right thing to say. Unfortunately, when I do open my mouth, the words that come out aren't the ones I should be saying.

"Would you like to come in?" There are so many reasons why he should say no, but him being here feels so right. I feel so safe when he's beside me, and I'm not ready to lose that just yet.

He looks down at himself and pulls his once pristine white t-shirt from his body. "I should probably go home and shower."

He's right. He should. But, fuck if I don't want to demand he stays exactly as he is because he looks so damn hot.

"I've got a shower," I blurt out, then bite down on my bottom lip to stop anything else spewing from my mouth.

"Oh yeah?" He takes a step forward, closing

the space between us. His heat burns my front, making my body ache to feel him pressed up against me.

"Yeah, I mean, it's pretty crap and kinda cold but...it's still a shower." His arm lifts and his fingers thread into my hair, pulling me closer to him. There's barely an inch between us. My head's tilted back so I can look up into his eyes as they bounce between mine and my lips. I don't think I've ever wanted to be kissed quite so badly.

I'm a second away from throwing caution to the wind and reaching up for his lips when he pulls away and says, "Lead the way."

I don't hesitate in lifting my arm, unlocking my front door and pushing it open. The sound of his heavy footsteps tells me he's following and taking in the sparse state of my flat.

"I'm sorry, it's not—"

I turn, but the sight of him standing there staring at nothing but me takes my breath. This place is tiny, but with him here, sucking all the air out of it, we could be inside a cupboard, not a studio.

"Don't apologise, Quinn. It's more than I've got, I can assure you of that."

I don't think for a moment that can be true, but I nod anyway.

"The bathroom's behind that door. The washing machine doesn't work, but if you throw your clothes out, I can rinse them in the sink and pop them in the dryer for you."

Without even thinking about it, he reaches behind his head and pulls the fabric of his t-shirt up his body.

My lips part and my eyes drop to take in the skin he's revealed. It's toned and tanned with just the perfect amount of hair covering his chest.

The temperature inside my small flat suddenly feels scorching as he throws his shirt towards me. I just about manage to catch it, unable to drag my eyes from his half-naked body.

His hands drop to his waistband as he toes off his boots, discarding them where they are. He drops his trousers and pulls off his socks. He stuff them back into his boots and throws the trousers on the top.

"Leave them," he says, flicking his eyes to the pile of clothes. "Just do that."

Then, as if getting almost naked in a stranger's flat is normal, he turns and heads towards the bathroom door.

I stay exactly where I am, frozen to the spot as the sound of the water running hits my ears and steam begins to bellow from the room. He didn't even shut the bloody door. As if I need that kind of temptation. My need to strip down and follow him is already quite strong.

CHAPTER NINE

REALISING that I can't still be standing in the same spot when he reappears, I squeeze the fabric in my hands and will the image of water cascading down over his muscular arms from my head. I don't need those kinds of thoughts in my mind if I want to get through this evening without making a mistake I can't take back. I throw his shirt into the sink and slip my coat from my shoulders.

Without thinking, I run the water to fill the sink and throw in a scoopful of powder before a shout fills the room.

"Argh, what the fuck? Turn the tap off, it's fucking freezing."

"Shit, sorry." I can't help but laugh as I reach for the tap to stop the water. I live here on my own;

I have no reason to know that running the tap makes the shower run cold. I don't tend to do both at the same time.

Making the most of the water that's still in the kettle, I boil it and throw it into the cold water. Forcing myself to focus on the task in hand, I set about rinsing his t-shirt and lose myself watching the water turn a dirty grey colour. When the shower has stopped, I run a clean bowl of water to rinse it out with, trying like hell to ignore the fact that he's about reappear at any moment.

I wring out as much water as I can when a shiver runs down my spine. My muscles ache for me to turn around, but I'm scared of what I'll find when I do.

Sadly, the first words that leave his lips have me moving without any thought.

"What the fuck are you wearing?"

I spin around so fast that water from his still sopping shirt covers me. "Shit," I mutter, turning and throwing it back into the sink.

Heat seeps into my back before his finger runs around the neck of my cardigan. Goosebumps prick my skin as I wait to find out what he's going to do next.

"I thought you wanted to banish the little old lady clothes."

"I-I do. B-but, they're all I had."

"Then I think another shopping trip is in order, because these aren't who you are." He couldn't be saying truer words. These clothes have never been me, just fabric that I hid behind for everyone else's sake. "I think they need to go."

His fingers slip around my waist until he finds the buttons running down my front. As he pops each one open, my breathing increases. By the time he's at the top, my chest is heaving, my breaths coming out in needy pants. Wrapping his tattooed fingers around the fabric at my shoulders, he slowly pulls it down my arms.

"Joe." It's meant to come out as a warning, but it sounds like a needy moan for more even to my own ears.

His heat is almost scalding as he closes the space between us, his front lining up with my back. The obvious thickness of his length presses into my arse, and my teeth sink into my bottom lip to stop me from making any more embarrassing noises.

My heart thunders in my chest, and my veins fill with fire as his lips brush against the curve of my neck.

"Let me take it all away."

"W-what?" I stutter.

"Whatever it is that puts fear in your eyes. Whoever it is you keep looking over your shoulder for. The reason you're hiding."

"I-I'm n-not—"

"Shhh...don't lie to me, Quinn. I can see it all. I can feel it. Allow me to make you forget, just for an evening."

"Oh god," I moan as his lips continue their trail up my neck. How am I supposed to say no to that?

"I haven't been able to forget about you. Just the memory of you melting in my hands last night has kept me hard all day."

"We can't." My words are barely a whisper, showing just how weak my argument is.

"Says who? Mr. Boring?" His hands move from my waist and find the hot skin of my stomach as he lifts my cami. There's no way he misses my body's tremble when our skin connects. "Get out of your head, Quinn. What does your body want? Listen to what your body needs."

"Fuck." As I turn in his arms, he takes one look at my face and his lips are on mine. He wastes no time in sliding his tongue past my parted lips and seeking my own to dance with.

One of his hands splays out across my back and ensures we're pressed as tightly together as possible while the other dives into my hair as he devours my mouth like he'd die without it.

It's the single best kiss of my life. He makes me feel needed, wanted and desirable—all things I've never experienced before on this kind of level.

"I need you so fucking bad, Quinn. You're driving me fucking crazy," he mutters against my jaw as he kisses along it and down my neck.

"So take me. Do what you promised. Make me forget."

He walks me backwards until I bump up against the counter. His fingers grasp the hem of my cami, but before he pulls it up and over my head, he looks to me for permission. My chest swells that he's thoughtful enough to do so, and heat floods my core at the dark and dangerous look in his eyes. But it's not the bad kind of dangerous. It's the incredibly sexy and full of wicked promises kind.

I nod, and he wastes no time in pulling it off me and throwing it over his shoulder. His lips drop to the swell of my breasts and he kisses, licks and nips along the edge of my bra. My breasts swell with my need for more and strain against the fabric, desperate for more attention. Slipping his fingers inside the lace, he pulls the cup down and wastes no time in feasting on my puckered nipple.

My head falls back as sparks of pleasure shoot to my core and threaten to buckle my knees. Sucking my peak deep into his mouth, his teeth bite down so just the right amount of pain mixes with the pleasure. My fingers grip the counter, my nails digging in the underside of the wood.

"More. I need more."

His eyes flick up to mine, desire and delight shining back at me. The fabric around my ribs is released, and in one swift move my bra joins the collection of clothing on the floor.

"You think I can get you off like this again?"

I don't get a chance to respond, because his large hands cup my breasts and he sets to work.

In no time, my core is clenching as his ministrations on my breasts bring me closer and closer to my release. He's alternated between pinching my nipples with his thumb and forefinger and teasing with his tongue and teeth.

"You taste so fucking sweet. I can't wait to discover more."

"Yes," I breathe, desperate for everything he can give me. "Yes, yes." He ups the ante, pinching harder, biting deeper, and I fall. I fall into a mind-numbing bliss, but it only lasts so long because I need him inside me, surrounding me, everywhere.

Lifting up, his fingers wrap around my neck as his lips land on mine. The move is possessive, and I can't get enough. At this very moment, I can't think of anything better than being his.

His tongue plunges into my mouth as my hands find the sculpted skin of his back. My nails run down until I hit the towel that's somehow still wrapped around his waist. The need to pull it from his body is all consuming, and just as I'm about to do it, his hands drop to the waist of my skirt. The feeling of the zip being lowered has my thighs clenching.

I should be embarrassed about my utterly unsexy underwear, but, just like my bra, Joe doesn't even bat an eyelid as my skirt drops around my ankles and he quickly pulls my tights in the same direction, dropping to his knees before me.

When he sits back on his haunches and looks up at me, all I see is lust and need reflected back at me.

My chest heaves as our eye contact holds, a silent conversation passing between us. I start to think he's not going to move until he quickly stands and lifts me so I've no choice but to throw my arms around his shoulders and wrap my legs around his waist.

His length that's tenting the towel presses between my legs and gives me just a taste of what's still to come. My core clenches with anticipation.

"Bed?" Joe asks, spinning on the spot.

"Sofa. It unfolds."

"Fuck it."

He drops me onto the sofa and pulls me so I'm practically hanging off the edge. Landing on his knees, he drags my knickers down my thighs and throws them into the room. His eyes zero in on my centre and my thighs close under his close scrutiny. If I'd have known this was going to happen, I might have spent a little longer pruning down there.

"Don't," he barks, pressing his large, calloused hands against the soft skin of my thighs and pushing my legs as wide as they'll go. "You're beautiful. Every inch of you."

Heat hits my cheeks and makes its way down my neck and onto my chest.

"Don't believe me? Let me show you." His lips hit the inside of my thigh and he kisses up from my knee until he's at my core. He licks at my seam before finding my clit and teasing it with the perfect amount of pressure. It's like he knows exactly how to play my body, despite this being the first time he's touched me.

My back arches and my toes curl when he dips his tongue inside me.

"Holy shit." Why haven't I experienced this before? I force the thought from my head, not wanting any part of my past tainting this.

His tongue finds my clit again, and his finger teases at my entrance. He circles and dips inside just enough to have me pleading with him for more. I've never begged a man for anything in my life, but this right now feels so natural.

He sucks hard on my clit, his fingers diving inside me until he hits an undiscovered part of me that has me barreling towards the most intense release I've ever experienced. Lights flash behind my eyes as my fingers grip his hair with such strength I swear I'm gonna rip it from his head.

"Joe," I squeal, not giving a crap how loud I am as wave after wave of pleasure takes over my body.

He continues until tmy body stops pulsating before sitting back on his heels with a smug as fuck smile on his face.

I push up on my palms, ready to say something about it, but my naked body catches my eye and I realise I'm sitting here with my legs spread, everything on show while he's still got that damn towel around his waist.

He glances down at what's holding my attention before standing directly in front of me, his crotch right in my eyeline. His excitement is obvious with the tenting of the fabric, and my mouth waters to see all of him.

"Go on then." One side of his mouth curls up. His arrogance is enough to have me reaching out and wrapping my fingers around the towel.

In one quick movement, I pull it from his body.

My eyes fly to his cock and my chin drops. *Jesus.* My mouth waters, and I'm powerless to stop my tongue sneaking out and licking my bottom lip.

It's not the first time I've seen one, but fuck, it's the first time I've seen one quite like that. He's pierced.

My hand moves to reach out, but my insecurity gets the better of me.

"Uh…" My eyes fly up to his, but I find no hesitation. He knows exactly what he's doing, and I'd be lying if I said that wasn't a turn on.

He lunges forward, his hand cradling the back of my head as he lays me down on the sofa. His lips find mine as his hard cock teases between my legs, making my muscles clench to experience just how he's going to feel inside me.

I might be naive with my lack of experience in this department, but even I know that piercing is meant to feel incredible. He's already proven himself to be way more skilled than my previous partner, so I can't help but hope that it's going to be mindblowing.

"Joe, please," I moan, needing more than this delicious torture.

Reaching over the end of the sofa, he grabs his discarded trousers and pulls a condom from his pocket.

My eyes lock on his cock as he rolls it down his shaft like he's done it a million times. *He probably has,* a little voice says in the back of my mind, but the second he rubs the head through my wetness, all thoughts leave my mind in favour of the pleasure he can bring me.

"Take it slow, yeah?" I whisper, embarrassed that I even need to say it, but it's been longer than I'm willing to admit.

"Shit, are you a—" His eyes widen, although I'm not sure if it's with delight or terror.

"No, no. Just...uh...inactive?" I don't mean for

it to come out as a question, but my word of choice sounds weird even in my own head.

"Well, let's put an end to that, shall we?"

He doesn't give me a chance to respond. Instead, he pushes slowly inside me. My walls stretch to accommodate him, my entire body sighing with relief.

"Fuck." His voice is deep and filled with disbelief. His muscles strain as he holds himself back. "So fucking good."

He pushes deeper, and I gasp when he finds the same spot he did with his fingers that made me fly.

"Move, Joe. Please." I'm begging, but I don't care. I need this right now.

"Thought you'd never ask." He winks before slipping his hands under my arse and lifting me just so. The head of his cock and the piercing graze that spot, sending a shudder down my spine.

His hand runs up my thigh, up and over my stomach before pinching my nipples and finally wrapping around my neck.

With our eyes locked, he pulls almost all the way out of me before pushing straight back in. He does it over and over, increasing the tempo every time until I'm clawing at his back and crying out for more.

I'm pretty sure I've never made a noise during sex before, but suddenly it's all I can do to keep my mouth shut.

A fine sheen of sweat begins to bead Joe's brow as his movement gets more and more erratic.

"Come on me, Quinn. All over my cock." His words are no more than a gutteral groan, but I hear every single one loud and clear, and fuck if they don't push me that little closer to finding my release.

His fingers release my neck. I want to complain about the loss, but then his thumb presses against my clit and I lose all train of thought as my release hits me out of nowhere and totally consumes me.

No longer able to keep my eyes open, my lids lower as they roll back in my head in pleasure, my body twitching and sucking him deeper as I ride out the waves.

"Fuck. Fuck. Fuuuuck," he moans before he stills, his cock twitches, and he lets go of his own orgasm.

He drops on top of me, his softening cock still inside me as our chests heave and our increased breaths mingle.

"Fuck, Quinn. That was…" He doesn't finish his thought. Instead, his lips find mine and he shows me just how much he enjoyed it.

Flipping us over, he somehow manages not to allow us both to end up on the floor. He settles back with me on his lap, his cock slipping free at last. As he reaches down to pull the condom off, I attempt to stand.

"Where the hell are you going?"

"To…uh…clean up?" I awkwardly wrap my arms around my breasts in an attempt to hide from him. It was fine when he had his hands on me, but now I feel totally naked.

"I'm not done with you yet."

"Oh?" My eyes widen.

"There's another condom in my pocket. I intend on using it before either of us puts clothes on." Hesitantly, I walk over and drop down beside the fabric. "Go on," he encourages.

With the little silver packet between my thumb and forefinger, I stand and look at where he's fisting his already hard cock.

"Again?"

"Fucking right. Get over here."

As I climb onto his lap, his hands run up my

back and pull me forward until my nipples brush against the light covering of hair on his chest.

I shudder.

"So sensitive." His hands slip around to take their weight, and he palms and pinches until my chest is heaving once again.

With his lips attached to the skin of my neck, he rolls on the second condom without even looking.

"Now, ride me."

I look down at the thickness of his cock, standing proud from his body, and my legs quiver.

Scooting forward a little, I lift up until he lines the head of his cock with my very ready entrance.

"Slow," he demands, and I'm powerless but to do as he says.

I hiss as he fills me, hitting all my over-sensitive nerves. My pussy twitches and clenches as another release makes itself known. I knew it was possible, but I never imagined I'd ever be with a man who could drag this kind of pleasure from my body.

"Now, kiss me. I need your lips."

With our tongues duelling, I manage to find my rhythm with the help of his hands on my hips.

It feels like no time before my thighs are trembling, ready for another release.

"Let go," he whispers in my ear. "Let me feel you."

If I thought the last one knocked me for six, then this orgasm tilted my fucking world on its axis. I don't know whether it's the position or what, but before it's even finished, I know it's the exact thing I need in my life right now.

His hips thrusts up into me as my body grows limp above him before he bites down on the skin covering my collarbone and rides out his own release.

I fall forward onto his chest, and his arms wrap around me.

I'm sated, relaxed, and so fucking comfortable.

CHAPTER TEN

IT TAKES me a few minutes to figure out where I am and what's happening when my eyes flutter open. The bulb above my head is on, bathing the flat in light, but I was asleep on the sofa.

The sound of breathing hits my ears, and I panic.

Jumping from the sofa—and from his hold, it seems—I swipe the first item of clothing I find from the floor and hold it against my naked body.

Joe drags his eyes open and looks at me standing in front of him on the verge of a panic attack.

"You need to leave."

"I...uh...what?"

"You need to leave. Right now."

"But—"

"No buts, Joe. This can't happen. This shouldn't have happened. I'm your…" I can't bear to say the word. "I'm your *teacher*." I've no idea why I whisper it; it's not like anyone's going to overhear.

"Too late now, babe. It's happened, and I'm more than ready for it to happen again."

He glances down, and when I follow his gaze I find his cock, hard again.

Jesus.

"I can't do this, Joe. I can't lose the only thing I have left in my life. I can't and I won't because of some stupid mistake."

"Mistake?" he asks, getting up from the sofa, his eyes hardening at my choice of word.

"It shouldn't have happened."

"But it did, and don't tell me you didn't feel it."

"Feel what?" I feign innocence.

"The connection. Us. The chemistry."

Oh, I felt it all right. I have since that first day he walked into my classroom. I should have been stronger, should have been able to ignore it. But I couldn't, and now look at me—standing with his disgusting trousers wrapped around my body which smells like him and sex.

Touching him was forbidden. I knew that. But I did it anyway. As if my life isn't already one big clusterfuck—I've just added another load of drama to it.

"Quinn, please. Just come back to bed."

"It's not a bed, Joe. It's a sofa, and the fact that I don't even have a bed should prove just how fucked up my life is. Trust me when I say that this is the last place you should want to be."

Standing, he takes a few steps towards me, but I take the same back.

"Talk to me. Tell me. Let me help you, whatever it is. You don't need to fight it alone."

"No. I can't."

"I'm right here, Quinn. Tell me what you need."

Emotion threatens to climb up my throat, but I swallow it down. I need to be strong if I'm going to convince him that I'm doing the right thing. "I need you to leave. This can't happen again."

"This is bullshit, Quinn, and you know it." His arms fly up in disbelief, and I cower away. "What the fuck? Quinn, I wouldn't...I'd never...Fuck." His eyes widen in shock, his fingers threading in his hair and tugging painfully hard.

"Just get out, please. I need to be alone."

His eyes are wide and focused on me as he debates what to do.

"Please, Joe."

With a regretful nod of his head, he tugs his boxers on before turning to me and holding out his hand. I stupidly think he's asking for me, and I almost cave. My arm twitches to reach out and wrap my fingers around his, but after a second I realise that he just wants his trousers.

I pull the fabric from around me and hand it over. Broken and defeated, I allow my arms to drop to my sides. I'm sending away the one good thing in my life; what more do I really have to worry about?

Once he's dressed in what's available, seeing as his sopping wet t-shirt is still in the sink, he steps up to me. His fingers slide into my hair and his lips press against my forehead.

We stand like that for the longest time with just our breaths filling the silent space around us. He might not be saying any words, but I can't help feeling like he's making promises. I already know they're not ones he can keep.

"This isn't over, Quinn."

With those words ringing in my ears, he releases me and walks from the flat.

The second the door shuts behind him, all the air leaves my lungs.

What the fuck did I just do?

Without even looking at the sofa where only minutes ago I was sleeping in his arms, I run towards the bathroom. I turn the shower on and allow the steam to fill the small room as I rest my palms on the basin and hang my head.

I just sent away the one person with the ability to make me forget. To make me feel safe. To make me feel alive.

I know it might be the right thing to do—I can't lose my career; it's the only thing I have right now —but fuck, this hurts.

I lift one hand to my chest and rub at the ache which is only getting worse the longer I'm alone. My hand trembles, and I try to ignore it. I'm used to the fear. It's what's got me this far, and I refuse to give into it now. I'm not stupid—I know that what I've already been through has been the easy bit. What I've got to come is only going to be harder.

Risking a look at myself in the steamed up mirror in front of me, I let out a sigh of frustration.

I look like the woman I've always wanted to be. I've got the hair, the make up, some of the clothes

I've always dreamed of, but still my past holds me back. Will it always be this way? Will they always have this hold on me? Will I always be forced to live by the fucked up rules and ideals even when I'm miles away?"

I stare into eyes I don't recognise and pray to whomever might be listening that after what I did, I'll be free. That's all I want. To be free to live the life I've always coveted. A life in which the decisions I make are mine and mine alone.

I've had a taste of it. *He* allowed me a taste, and now I want it more than ever. I'm like a junkie craving my next hit, only the thing I'm craving is what most other people have. A life of their own.

"Fuck," I bark, slamming my hand down on the porcelain in front of me.

Every muscle in my body aches for me to go running after him, to demand that he returns and holds me, holds my hand through what's to come, but I know I can't. And not just because of my career, but because I can't do it to him. I've no doubt he can handle it, but he shouldn't have to. My past is mine to bear; it shouldn't weigh down anyone else. It's already destroyed too many lives.

I hate to do it, but I step into the shower and allow the water to wash away what's left of Joe. His scent rinses from my body as the tears I'd been holding but refusing to cry stream down my face. I learned years ago that it was safe to let it all go when standing under a torrent of water.

The longer I stand there, the weaker my body feels. I've not nearly had enough sleep in the last forty-eight hours, and I'm struggling, especially after the orgasms.

My back hits the cold tiles behind me, but I barely feel it against my numb skin as I slide down to the shower tray at my feet. The water continues to trickle over me as images from my past that I'd rather not remember run through my mind, reminding me why I ran when I got an opportunity.

***

MY BODY FEELS like it's going to explode as Joe thrusts inside me, his large calloused hands squeezing my breasts as he demands for me to come. My chest heaves as I race closer and closer to the release he wants from me. I'm just about to fall when another face appears as he relentlessly slams into me, over and over until I'm raw.

"Fucking bitch, why won't you come? Are you fucking broken?"

I fight to keep the tears that are burning my eyes inside as I keep up the facade he expects—that everyone expects—of me.

I moan, hoping it sounds convincing before calling out his name. Bile rushes up my throat at hearing it, but I've come to know it's the only way to make it stop.

His cock pulses inside me, filling me, trying to force me to give him a son to continue his masochistic ways.

Chance will be a fine thing.

I think of those little pills I keep hidden in the lining of my handbag. There's no way I'll give that man a baby. I'd rather he killed me before I subjected a kid to the kind of life we live here.

I SUCK in a deep breath and sit up. My hand covers my racing heart as the surroundings come into focus.

It was just a dream. *Just a dream?* A fucking nightmare, more like.

Realising it's almost lunchtime, I drag my

aching body from the sofa I never bothered converting into a bed when I fell onto it last night. I had plans for this weekend. I wanted to be brave and go out and explore. Joe had given me the confidence to embrace my new city, and I was desperate to see some of the sights I've only been able to enjoy from a photograph, in a magazine or on the TV up until now, but sitting here with the winter sun shining in through my little window, the last thing I want to do is go out.

A tingle of fear races down my spine as I think about my nightmare. I haven't had one since I left. I thought I'd managed to escape that little bit of my past, but it seems that now I've sent away the one thing that made me feel safe, he's going to slip back into my brain to torture me some more. It doesn't matter how many miles I put between us, he'll always be inside my head, and he damn well knows it. That was all part of the game. The game he played with me, and with his students. If only I was brave enough to speak up sooner, to expose him for what he really is.

Heading for the kettle for a very strong cup of coffee, my eyes land on the wet fabric still in the sink, and my stomach twists painfully as memories of his face as I made him walk away fill my mind.

I drain the now very cold water and set about washing it once again, wishing like hell it was last night again and that he's going to come strolling out of the bathroom wrapped in only a towel.

I know it's not going to happen, and disappointment floods me until the back of my throat burns with tears.

I did the right thing. I did the right thing, I repeat over and over, trying to convince myself that it's the truth.

I need to get through this alone, and then, when it's safe to properly move on, I will. I will rebuild my life the way I want, but right now isn't the time to be focusing on my future. I need to focus on the present and what might be waiting just around the corner for me.

Throwing Joe's shirt into the dryer, I find my own dirty clothes, intending on giving them the same treatment seeing as a trip to the laundrette is the last thing I want to do right now. The monotonous task of hand-washing them is actually quite tempting, but when I glance down at the twinset in my hands, something rebellious hits me and instead of dropping them into the warm water I've just run, I ball them up and throw them in the bin.

Instead, I wash the few new bits I've bought and throw what I can into the dryer before grabbing my phone and doing some online shopping.

I plan next week and order the food I need. I keep the purchases to the minimum, knowing that I've got other things I want to splash what little money I have on. God, pay day can't come soon enough.

I get through three cups of coffee, but by the time I eventually put my phone down, I've not only got my food arriving tomorrow but three separate clothes deliveries. I've kept some of the old me hanging around for too long. It's time to banish the weak and pathetic woman she was and finally embrace the life I've always dreamed of, even if it is from the comfort of my studio flat.

I want to be braver than this. I want to be out embracing the city and exploring some of what Joe gave me a taste of on Thursday night, but after what happened with him yesterday and then my nightmare, I'm not sure I can do it. I'll have to leave eventually—I have a job, after all. I tell myself that I've got two days to wallow about the ridiculous mistake I made inviting Joe in here last night and in memories of my past before I take London by storm on Monday morning.

Okay, so that might be a bit of an exaggeration, but it fires me up enough to push my past back behind the trapdoor I thought I'd banished it to.

CHAPTER ELEVEN

I HOLD my head up high as I walk out of my building first thing on Monday morning. I'm wearing one of the new outfits I ordered over the weekend, I've done my hair and make-up, and I'm feeling good. But that doesn't stop me looking around the second the door slams shut behind me. I pause to see if there's any movement or rustling in the bushes.

I'm being paranoid, I know I am, but I can't help it. Joe pulling up on the curb like he did in front of me Friday night really spooked me.

I tell myself that no one's there, that no one even cares where I am, and I head towards the tube. I feel better once I'm surrounded by commuters and heading to my classroom.

My first lesson of the week is with Jodi. I'm hopeful that her last lesson was just a one off, and I'll find her smiling and more willing to interact, but the second she walks into the room, I know it was wishful thinking.

She keeps her head down as the others chat away and slowly find their seats. She pulls her books out but still doesn't risk glancing up. My heart aches for her. I've no idea what her story is, but there's something so sad and broken in her eyes, ones I recognise from my former life. I desperately want to tell her that it won't last forever, that she is in control of her own destiny, but it's not really my place to just assume. People's lives are often much more complex than we can imagine, and I'd hate to jump to conclusions about what she's dealing with.

The students must have had a good weekend, because it seems to take forever to get them settled. Eventually, I get them reading silently so I can begin catching up with their coursework progress.

Flipping my planner to this class, I start at the top and make my way down the register, talking individually to each student.

"Jodi, you're up," I call.

She pushes her chair out and walks towards the

front of the room. No one looks up at her; it's kind of like she's invisible, probably exactly how she wants it.

She sits herself down in the chair opposite and drops her work to my desk. I scan over it, getting a feel for the quality, and I can't believe what I'm looking at.

"Jodi, this is amazing. Your use of language is incredible, and the way you're describing how that sonnet made you feel...it's well beyond the level of this class. You're really talented."

Looking up from the paper, I watch as her sad, lonely face morphs into the most stunning smile.

"Really?" she asks, her voice barely above a whisper.

"Yeah, really."

"I wasn't sure if it was right."

"There's no wrong answer to how a passage makes you feel, Jodi. That will be different for every one of us based on our lives and experiences. It's the way you've described it."

The pure joy on her face melts my heart. This right here is why I wanted to be a teacher. I grew up knowing I didn't really have any other choice, but I truly enjoy what I do. Although I've imagined my ideal life a million times, I was always still teaching. I love giving young people the opportunity to find themselves just like Jodi is right now.

"Have you thought about a writing career?"

She's silent as she thinks, and it's then that she pushes up the sleeves of her jumper. My eyes drop at the movement, and my mouth gapes at the dark blue and purple bruises that encircle her wrists.

"Jodi?"

In a rush, she pulls her sleeves back down. "It's nothing," she mutters. "I...uh...just fell."

I don't say anything. She doesn't need me to point out that she's quite obviously lying.

Pushing the chair out behind her, she grabs her work and races back to her seat, her head back down in defeat.

My heart aches for what she's going through and my hands tremble, having experienced first-hand the fear she must feel. Obviously, I'm going to report it at the first opportunity I get—much to Jodi's horror, I'd imagine—but other than that, all I can really do is be here and help her get the qualifications she needs to improve her life.

Thoughts of Jodi and how I can help her consume my mind for the rest of the lesson. I've refused to look at my phone since I placed my orders on Saturday, but I know there are emails from Joe waiting for me. I'm just not ready to deal with the reality of what I did Friday night.

Thanks to him, my nightmares are back full force. I've had hardly any sleep since I kicked him out. Every time I shut my eyes, *he's* there. It's not bad enough that my memories of him never leave—he's got to disrupt my slumber now, too.

Jodi glances up at me as everyone else leaves the room. Her eyes are begging for me to let this go, but we both know that I can't.

"Jodi, wait," I call and watch her shoulders sink. "I'm here, okay? If you need anything."

"Thank you," she mutters before basically running for the door.

Falling down on my desk, I rest back in the chair, wishing I could just take a little nap before my next class.

A knock sounds out around the room, and I'm forced to drag my heavy head up.

"Yes?" I call, expecting a student to come running back in because they'd forgotten something. But when the door opens, something very different emerges. A wicker basket.

"This was just delivered for you," Caroline, our department admin says, walking over and dropping the basket to my desk. "I'm assuming you're not expecting it from the look on your face."

"No, I'm really not." As I stare at the box, reality starts to find its way through my confusion, and my heart begins to race. Is this a joke? Has he found me? Is it going to explode when I open it? Crazy thoughts start running through my head as Caroline stands awkwardly, obviously waiting for me to open it to discover what's hiding inside. "Thank you for bringing it in for me."

"You're welcome." She rocks back and forth awkwardly on her feet. It's not until I turn towards my computer that she gets the message that I'm not opening it in front of her, and she starts to back away from my desk.

It's not until she's closed the door behind her that I reach out and slide the box across the desk.

I open the folded tag, but inside all it says is *Ms Quinn Smith*. My hands tremble as I undo the buckles holding it closed, and I brace myself for what I find.

"What the hell?" Pulling the lid open, I find it full of luxury girly products. Letting go of the lid, I start taking them out one at a time. Hand soap and lotion, bubble bath, candles, face masks, moisturiser, the list goes on. It's not until I get to the last item that's wrapped in soft pink tissue that I know for a fact who it's from. It's two ceramic signs, one with *No Regrets* and the other *Live Life Your Way* written in a script font across the front.

Tears burn up my throat until they hit the back of my eyes. Without even thinking about it, I know this is the sweetest thing anyone has ever done for me.

My eyes are still full of unshed tears when my next class arrives. I attempt to swallow down the emotion he caused as I slide the basket under my desk. I glance at my handbag, knowing that my phone is right there. I've probably got a million emails from him. I should look and thank him for the gift, but I know that by replying he'll want more. I've already made a huge mistake when it comes to him, and I think I might be safer avoiding him and keeping our contact limited to Thursday nights in class. It might be the last thing I want in reality, but it's all I can do right now.

THE BASKET and my phone taunt me for the rest of the day. I stay a little later than I'd originally planned so that I can report what I've learned about Jodi, and by the time I leave, it's completely dark outside.

The second I was alone, I woke my computer up and found my emails.

I ignored everything in my inbox and opened up a new one. Finding the name of the woman who deals with all the college's safeguarding, I began my email about Jodi.

I hate that she's going to think I'm sticking my nose in by doing this. She's inevitably going to be called in for a meeting following the information I'm about to pass on, and she's going to hate it.

If her home situation is anything like I'm imaging, then she does everything she can to hide and being pulled up and put on the spot is going to be her worst nightmare—aside from whoever it was who put those bruises on her.

I flexed my fingers a few times before they stopped shaking enough to allow me to type properly.

"I really hope this helps in the long run, Jodi," I whispered to myself and got everything I'd seen and felt into the email in the hope that her life can turn a corner because of it.

Pulling my coat tighter around myself, I turn to look to my right. There's a white van idling on the double yellow lines out the front of the building. My heart jumps into my throat. He's waiting for me?

He's staring down at his phone so misses the fact I've left the building. Without putting much thought into it, I bolt left and hope I'm lost in the crowd.

I race towards the tube, my entire body shaking with adrenaline.

The easiest thing to do would be to get into his van again. But it's dangerous. He's waiting for me right out the front of where I work. The very last place we need to be caught together. Not that there will be a chance of us being caught together, because there won't be a next time.

It's not until I'm locked in my flat that I relax. After placing the basket on my coffee table, I shrug off my coat and pull my boots from my legs. I find the spaghetti I ordered over the weekend and set about making myself some dinner.

While I'm waiting for it to cook, I have a moment of weakness and pull my phone from my bag.

Twenty-four emails.

Twenty-fucking-four.

No wonder he was waiting outside. He probably wanted to make sure I was still alive.

I ignore the first twenty-three and open the last one.

To: Quinn Smith
From: Tatstwatsandarseholes
Subject: Juliet, Juliet, wherefore art thou Juliet

Dear Miss Smith
I sincerely apologise if I've done something to upset you.
I want to make it up to you.
Your carriage awaits...
Yours,
Mr. Kingsman

Checking the time of the email, I see that he sent it only five minutes before I saw him. I wonder if he's still there waiting for me? Or worse, would Eddie have seen him, or will he come here next?

Deciding the best outcome would be if I replied and stopped him turning up here, I start typing.

To: Tatstwatsandarseholes

From: *Quinn Smith*
Subject: *Not meant to be...*

Dear Mr. Kingsman,
Thank you for the gift basket. It is beautiful. I'm sorry, but this Juliet isn't to be rescued. Best we leave it now before the tragic ending.
Regards,
Miss Smith

I let out a giant sigh and drop my phone onto the sofa beside me. Really, those words are the last ones I want to say to him. In reality, I want to be begging him to come over here and keep me safe, but that's both unfair on him and the beginning of the end of my career.

Maybe he could change courses? I shoot down the little voice in my head who's getting carried away with herself. I've no reason to think that whatever has happened between us isn't more than a bit of fun to him. For all I know, his friends have dared him to bed the teacher.

My cheeks heat at the thought of being nothing more than a pawn in his games, but something tells me it's more than that, which is another reason why I need to stay away. The last thing I need right now as I try to rebuild my life is a serious relationship.

This is meant to be about me.

About me experiencing all the things I never got to, not falling for the first guy I laid eyes on.

After double-checking my phone is on silent, I finish off my dinner. I'm tempted all night to see if he's responded, but I tell myself that I'm not really avoiding him if I'm waiting for a reply.

CHAPTER TWELVE

BY THE TIME Thursday rolls around, I'm almost at breaking point. On Tuesday, I had a box of doughnuts delivered to work. Caroline once again hung around a little too long after delivering them —I'm not sure if she wanted to know who sent them or if she just wanted one. Unfortunately for her, I'd overslept that morning and was starving. I'm not even ashamed to admit that I ate the entire lot before I turned my sofa into a bed that night.

On Wednesday, I didn't have any deliveries at work, but just as I was sitting down to eat my questionable looking ready meal, the buzzer in my flat went off and, at the other end, was a man delivering Chinese. The dishes were exactly the same as we had last Thursday, and, when I got to the bottom of the bag, I found a note. *If you need a hand eating all this, call me...* followed by his phone number. I must admit that after reading that, I did go and get my phone. I even got as far as typing his number in and saving it in my contacts. But at no point did I connect the call.

Not only did my fear of another nightmare keep me awake Wednesday night, but knowing I'd be seeing Joe in mere hours was enough to have my heart racing.

How was he going to act after everything that's happened between us? Would he just let it go, seeing as I've not responded to any of his little reminders that he still exists that he's sent this week?

By the time the clock ticks around to the beginning of his class, I'm a nervous wreck. I've planned loads of group and individual quiet activities so I don't have to talk much for fear of totally screwing it up.

I breathe a sigh of relief when he's not the first into the room. It gives me hope that maybe he won't show, although I know it's only wishful thinking. He might not always act like the most engaged student in the room, but having marked his work to date, I know he's taking this seriously.

I'm writing instructions on the board when the atmosphere changes. I don't need to turn around to know he's just walked in, and that he's looking right at me. I continue what I'm writing, trying to ignore the burning of his stare. Dread knots my stomach that he might not be being all too discrete about what—or who—is holding his attention. As if this week's not been hard enough, I really don't need suspicious students.

I keep my eyes locked on the board for longer than necessary, putting off the inevitable of turning around and finding him looking like the bad boy geek I've always dreamed of.

Blowing out a slow breath, I spin and cast my eyes over my students, who are all sitting in their seats and patiently waiting for class to start. I breathe a sigh of relief that they're not looking between the two of us like they suspect something.

I do everything I can to keep my eyes from the back of the room, but eventually the pull becomes too much and I look over. He's watching me, exactly like I knew he was, and the second our eyes lock it's like a baseball bat smashes me in the chest. His eyes shine with concern as he studies me. Guilt hits me for not thanking him for all the gifts I've received over the last few days. Suddenly, my reasons for staying away from him don't seem all that important as his body calls to mine.

Standing behind my desk and using it to stop me from walking directly over to him, I start the class. Words pour from my mouth, but none of them register in my brain. I could be telling them any kind of crap right now about Shakespeare and I'd be none the wiser.

All sets of eyes but one lower to get started on the task I've given them. That other set holds mine captive, making my heart rate increase and causing my temperature to soar. They drop from mine and take in my new outfit. Desire pulls at his features as he takes in the black prom style dress that clings to my breasts and makes my waist look much smaller than it actually is. My muscles pull tight as I fight the need to walk over to him.

I know I need to break the connection between us before one of the other students notices, we're already on borrowed time, but it's easier said than done—especially when he looks back up to me. Something crackles between us, and it hits me between the legs. Memories of how it felt having his hands on me Friday night slam into me, and my blush trails down my neck and onto my chest.

His lips curl up into a smirk, telling me that he

knows exactly where my thoughts are. Anger burns through me that he's so obviously taunting me in the one place he knows he can't.

I turn my back on him and drag in some much-needed air. I'm stronger than to let him break me. Maybe the old me wouldn't have been, but the new me definitely is.

When I turn back around, he's staring down at the pad of paper in front of him. Something still tingles just beneath my skin with him in close proximity, but, without his attention, at least I'm able to get on with my job.

I grab the stack of marked work on my desk, making sure his is at the bottom of the pile, and I head over to my first student to give them feedback.

With ten minutes left of the lesson, the only work I've got left to give feedback on is Joe's. My hand trembles as I glance over at him. He must feel my stare, because he immediately looks up. His eyes drop to the papers in my hand and a knowing grin appears. He knows exactly what I'm avoiding.

Sucking in some strength, I take a step forward and then pull out the empty chair next to him.

"Mr. Kingsman, I must say I really enjoyed marking this. You have a way with words. It flows easily and clearly shows your understanding on the beginning of the story."

"A way with words, huh? I thought my talents lie elsewhere, if I'm being honest. What would you say, Miss Smith?" he leans in and whispers the last sentence.

My stomach knots as I fight for something to say that won't encourage him.

"I think...that if you keep your head down and focus, you'll come out of this with a really good grade that will give you that step towards the career and life you want."

"What if there's something I want more?" He scans my face, committing each of my features to memory.

"Focus on your future, Mr. Kingsman. That's the reason you're here."

"What if she is my future?"

My stomach damn near falls from my body at his admission.

"Sorry...I uh..." I stutter, scrambling to get out of the chair and away from him. There's no doubt in my mind that he was deadly serious, and it scares me more than I want to admit.

This can't happen. He can't happen.

I finish up the lesson for the evening, give the

students their homework assignment for the following week and bid them farewell.

Joe's eyes never leave me as he slowly starts to pack away. It's clear he wants to hang back to talk to me, but I already know being alone with him is a very bad idea.

As students start to leave, I push my chair under my desk and follow them out. Just before I round the corner, I look back over my shoulder to find him staring at me with disappointment written all over his face.

As the majority of the students turn left so they can leave the building, I bolt right towards the toilets, but I don't get very far as I crash into a body.

Looking up, I find Eddie staring down at me with an amused smirk.

"I knew you wanted me," he says with a wink. My stomach twists as I pull myself from his grip.

"I'm so sorry, I just..."

I rush away from him, my heart hammering in my chest.

"I'm not that bad, am I?" he chuckles behind me, but I don't stop to say anything.

Lowering the toilet seat, I fall down on to it and drop my face into my hands. My life was meant to get simpler once I was away from my old life, but I fear I've only made it a hell of a lot more complicated and things are only going to get worse. Every day that passes I expect to receive a phone call, but as of yet, there's been nothing. I know these things take time, but for the sake of those I left behind, something needs to happen to stop lives being ruined more than they already have been.

I wait in the toilets long enough that I hope Joe will have given up and left.

I can feel the pounding of my heart all the way to my toes as I make the silent journey back towards my classroom to collect my stuff.

Poking my head into the room, I breathe a sigh of relief when it appears to be empty. I walk inside and head straight to my desk to collect my stuff when a dark figure in the corner, perched against the desk opposite mine, makes me scream.

"Fuck." My breath heaves as my body shakes. My fear is debilatating and renders me powerless for the couple of seconds it takes me to realise who is staring back at me with a deep frown lining his forehead.

It's Joe.

You're safe.

Breathe.

"Shit, Quinn. I didn't mean...are you okay?"

Tears burn my eyes and my bottom lip trembles. I really thought it was *him* waiting for me.

"I'm...I'm f-fine." My voice breaks on every word. "You need to leave."

Pushing from the desk, he stalks towards me. "You need to stop pushing me away, Quinn. Don't think I don't know that that's what you're doing."

"It's for your own good," I mutter, not willing to divulge any information as to why. Looking down at the floor, I try to avoid the connection that forms when we stare at each other. He'll see too much.

"You might think that, but I very much disagree. You're a nervous wreck. What's going on? Let me help." His hot fingers grip my chin lightly, and I'm forced to look back at him. My breath catches when I see the concern in his eyes.

"It's nothing."

"Bullshit," he snaps, making me jump.

"I'm here, willing to do anything to help you. Stop fighting it."

"I can't." Staring down at my feet, I feel myself

starting to crumble under his concerned stare, but he's not having any of it.

Bringing my face back to his, he leans down and brushes his lips against mine. I want to fight it —it's what I should do—but the second he touches me, I'm lost to anything but him and I sag into him, totally forgetting where I am.

His lips part and his tongue darts out in search of mine.

I'm just about to meet his when heavy footsteps fill my ears.

Fuck.

I jump back like I've been burned. Hurt covers Joe's face, but he soon looks toward the door when he hears what's stopped me. We can't be caught in here together.

I hold my breath, waiting for my potential visitor to make themselves known and see how this is going to play out. Eddie is already suspicious of the changes in me. The last thing I need is for him to discover that Joe, one of my students, is the cause.

My head starts to spin, but instead of stopping and entering the room whoever it is continues down the corridor.

I fall back against the desk behind me and suck in a few ragged breaths.

"Come on, let's get out of here. You hungry?"

I'm not really, but I'm also not ready to be alone again so I nod, collect up my stuff and follow him out of the building, hoping like hell we're not spotted together.

"Stop worrying. I'm just helping you with your bags." He smiles down at me and everything I've been worrying about, scared of, over the last few days melts away. *Why does he make me feel so safe?*

After dropping my bag in his van, he takes me to a burger restaurant a few streets away.

We're seated in a hidden corner at the back of the restaurant. I couldn't have chosen better seats if I'd tried.

The silence stretches out between us but at no point does he ask me about what's bothering me, and I couldn't be more grateful.

"No twinset today?" he asks with a laugh.

"No, I binned them."

"Oh?"

"They're not me anymore."

"Anymore?"

I shake my head, not willing to say anything else.

"So...have you had a good week?"

I can't help but burst out laughing at his question. "It's been fine."

"Fine?"

"Yeah. I mean, I have this secret admirer that keeps sending me gifts, so that's nice."

"Oh? Tell me about him. He sounds perfect."

"That might be pushing it. He's going after something he can't have. I'm not the person he thinks I am."

"And who's that?"

I sit back and think about his question for a few minutes. "I'm lost, Joe. I moved here not even two months ago with the intention of finding out who I am. Until I got here, all of my life was planned out for me and I followed along like a good little girl. This is my chance but—"

"You're scared."

"More than you know."

"I've been there, Quinn. I've been alone. I've been lost and not had a clue who I am. We're more alike than you realise."

"I don't believe that for a second. You're so sure of yourself. So confident in everything."

"Now I am, but only because I've worked hard to be that way. Quinn, listen." He reaches across the table and takes my hand in his. "Our pasts don't define who we are. We do that. Only you have the power to determine your future. What do *you* want for your future?"

"To be free." I slam my lips shut. Why is it that everything I'm trying to keep to myself just spews out of me when I'm with him?

"And how do you do that?"

"I don't know," I whisper honestly.

There isn't much more conversation between us as the waitress brings over our burgers. We eat in silence. I mostly keep my eyes down, afraid of how much he can read in them.

"Can I take you home?"

"Uh..."

"I'll just drop you off. I won't even get out of the van. I just need to know you're back safe."

I nod. "Okay."

He leads me back to where he'd parked, and I drop into his passenger seat.

"So what do you do exactly?"

"General builder. But I want more."

"What's more?"

"I'm not one hundred per cent. Quantity surveyor, maybe, but I'd need a degree most probably. I'm not sure if I've got that in me."

"Don't be so modest. Of course you can do it. You're more than capable."

"You've only been my teacher for a few weeks."

"We can pick out the ones who are going to succeed the minute students walk through the door, Joe. You've got it."

He beams at my praise, and my heart turns over. I think back to his question about the future, and I wonder seriously for the first time if there's a space for him in it.

Joe stands by his words and doesn't even switch the engine off, let alone get out of his van.

After thanking him, I jump out and grab my bags. His eyes follow me all the way to the front door of my building, and knowing he's right there means I don't even look over my shoulder before entering. I know I'm safe while he's here.

I give him a quick wave before allowing the door to shut behind me.

The first thing I do when I get up to my flat is to go to the window. Just as I suspected, he's still there. He's too far away to be able to see him, but it's long minutes before his van starts backing out of the space.

I turn my sofa into a bed and settle with a book when my phone rings. My first thought is that it's

Joe, but I soon realise that he doesn't have my number. There are only a couple of people who do, and right now I don't really want to hear from any of them.

Pulling it from my bag, I take a deep breath and look at the screen. *Detective Barker.* Fuck.

Part of me doesn't want to answer. That part would rather be blissfully unaware of what might be happening in my absence. But the part of me that's desperate to move on has me swiping the screen and lifting the phone to my ear.

"Hello?" My voice sounds weak even to my own ears.

"Good evening. This is Detective Barker. How are you?" His voice is over-the-top happy, and my stomach drops to my feet. It's all I need to hear to tell me that what's going to come next is going to rock my world once again.

"I'm...surviving."

He clearly misses the hesitation in my tone or refuses to hear it.

"That's good to hear, because I've got some news."

"Go on."

"The story has been leaked to the press." *Shit.* "I thought it was only fair to warn you that it will most probably hit the headlines tomorrow." My head spins, and white noise fills my ears. My chest heaves as I fight to drag in the air I need, but it's no use. Nothing fills my lungs, and I can't catch my breath.

I can vaguely make out the low timbre of Detective Baker's voice in the background, but I hear no more words as I fall onto the bed and count my breaths as a way to try to calm myself before this turns into a full-on panic attack.

Tomorrow morning, everyone is going to know. The lies and scandal I exposed will be common knowledge. That's good, I tell myself. *It's what I wanted. But where will that leave me?*

"Are you still there?"

"Yeah, yeah, I'm still here," I manage when the fog begins to lift enough to make out his words.

"Did you hear all of that?"

"Yeah."

"Okay, great. Well, like I said. If you hear anything from them, call me immediately, but I'm confident that you're safe where you are. They won't want to bring any more heat on their shoulders."

"Great. Thank you."

I disconnect the call and allow my hand to

drop between my knees as I try to process the little bit of what I heard.

I thought it was only fair to warn you that it will most probably hit the headlines tomorrow.

My hands tremble as I think about the consequences of the world knowing about my old life with all its betrayal and misplaced trust. My stomach turns over, and I worry I'm about to puke right here on my dirty floor, but thankfully a few deep breaths make it abate slightly.

CHAPTER THIRTEEN

I DON'T GET a wink of sleep. Every bang and creek within the building has my heart in my throat, thinking that my past is going to come crashing through my door to teach me a lesson of my own for betraying them.

I know the exact words I'd hear. *"We're family, princess. This is what happens when you go against your own."*

Bang.

The sound of someone's front door slamming is enough to have me jumping from the bed and backing into the corner as my heart races.

Tears burn my eyes, but I refuse to give in to the fear racing through my veins. I've made it this far. I've started a new life. They won't ruin it for me now.

I'm hyper aware of everything as I get ready for work, but I fight against my need to hide like a coward. I'm not the one in the wrong. Why should I be the one hiding?

I want to say that I hold my head high and walk from the building like I have no cares in the world, but that's far from the truth. In reality, my entire body trembles as terror takes a tight grip on my lungs.

They won't break me, I repeat over and over as I make my way down towards the tube station.

I probably look like a right nut case as my head darts from side to side and up and down the street, desperately trying to find out if I'm being watched or followed.

My skin tingles with awareness, but I'm sure it's more my own fears that cause it because I see no sign of anyone looking my way, let alone trailing me. I haven't since the day I moved here, but that doesn't mean I'm safe. I thought I was safe in my own home before—I had no idea what monsters I was living with.

Nothing about my day is unusual, but I still

find myself looking over my shoulder at every opportunity. I stay as far away from any newspapers, TV and radio as possible. I'm not ready to relive all of that again—not yet, anyway. I'm not stupid, I know I'm going to have to endure seemingly endless court cases about what I exposed, but I'll deal with that when the time comes.

I make the final part of my journey home from the tube station, my paranoia is at an all time high seeing as it's dark. It's so much easier to remain in the shadows out of sight. I reach for my phone to call Joe numerous times, knowing that I'll feel safe if he's by my side. But I need to do this alone.

By the time I push the main door open, I'm breathing like I've just run a marathon. I jog up the stairs, using the last of my energy before pushing the key in the lock and triple-checking that I secure everything behind me.

This place might not be much to most people, but it's become my sanctuary. Do I wish I had more? Of course. I've worked my whole life and saved every penny I could. I never imagined a time where I'd be forced to leave all of that behind. All I can hope is that when this is all over, I might see some of it once again.

My stomach rumbles, reminding me that I've

not eaten all day. Turning to the fridge, I pull it open and groan. I could really do with a little comfort food tonight, but all I've got staring back at me is a half-eaten tub of soup, stale bread, and a block of cheese. Not exactly what I'm craving.

The knowledge that my first paycheck hit my bank today rattles around my head, but I fight the urge to pick up my phone and order a takeaway. I've got more important things to buy.

In the end, I begrudgingly pull the soup from the fridge with a sigh.

The steaming bowl in my hands almost crashes to the floor when the buzzer rings out through the silent flat.

"Fuck." My chest heaves, my breaths racing past my lips.

I place the bowl down with trembling hands and hesitate. After debating whether to answer it or not for a few seconds, I eventually walk over on unsteady legs and press down the button. I figure if my past were to come knocking, then it's not likely to be so blatant as to ring my buzzer.

My assumptions are proved correct when Joe's voice fills the tiny space around me.

"Quinn, you there?" The concern is evident in his tone. I must have done an even worse job than I thought of appearing normal yesterday evening.

"Yeah, I'm here. What's up?"

"I was kinda hoping you'd invite me in and I could tell you."

"Oh, um..." I should say no. I should find out what he wants and send him on his way to enjoy his Friday night. I've already experienced his kind of night out, and I know he wouldn't be satisfied with two-day-old re-heated soup in my tiny studio.

No matter what my brain tells my body to do, it seems my arm has a mind of its own because I don't even realise that I've pressed the button down to unlock the front door and allow him entry into the building until he thanks me.

Before long, I hear his footsteps thundering up the stairs. The louder they get, the harder my heart beats.

You're playing with fire, the little voice in my head says.

Seconds before I know he's going to be standing the other side of the door, I rush towards my mirror, wipe the stray make up from under my eyes and run my fingers through my hair.

Even after all these weeks, I still hardly recognise the woman staring back at me. A little rush of excitement tingles through my veins at the reminder that I'm living my own life at last, even if I am waiting for it to come crashing down around my feet at any second.

My stomach tumbles when his loud, manly knock sounds out.

"Get it together, girl."

I shake out my arms and hope my paranoia vanishes along with my nerves.

I quickly unlock all the locks and in mere seconds I'm pulling the door open to reveal the man I can't get out of my head.

Only I've not met this version of him before.

Gone are the braces and crisp white shirt, and there are no dirty work clothes in sight. Tonight, he's dressed more casually in a pair of skinny dark jeans and a white polo shirt, although his glasses remain.

"You approve?" he asks, and my cheeks heat.

"Shit...I..." I stutter, my body frozen solid as his eyes burn into mine.

"Don't apologise. I like knowing what you're thinking."

His words immediately get my back up. I've been controlled my entire life by men who 'think' they know what I want and what I think.

I'm so done with that.

"You don't know me," I spit, much to his surprise if his raised eyebrows are anything to go by.

His hand lifts to rub the back of his neck, and I instantly feel awful for assuming he meant more than he did with his comment.

"Fuck, I didn't mean—"

"I'm sorry, it was my fault. Old habits die hard, I guess."

His brows draw together. I know he's desperate to discover more about my past, but I'm barely able to think about it right now without falling into a panic attack, let alone talk about it.

"Can I...?" he trails off and nods over my shoulder into my flat. My eyes follow, and I hesitate. "I promise I'm not going to jump you or anything. I just have a proposition that might interest you."

I narrow my eyes at him, already interested in his cryptic statement, and stand aside to allow him over the threshold.

"Coffee?" I ask, walking past where he's dropped to the sofa and over to the kitchen.

"Sure."

I put the kettle on and get the mugs out,

anything that will attempt to distract me from the pull that's always there when he's close.

Chancing a glance over my shoulder, I find him sitting back, relaxing on my sofa with his eyes locked on me. My need to find a seat on his lap is strong, but I fight to keep even a scrap of my self-control and continue with what I'm doing...but that's not before he graces me with a heart-stopping smile. That alongside the cheeky glint in his eyes makes me wonder what kind of proposition he's turned up here with.

"So?" I ask, placing his coffee down on the table and sitting as far away from him as possible on my small two-seater sofa.

"So..." He leans forward and places his elbows on his knees. His eyes never leave mine. "I get that you don't want to talk about it. Honestly, I do. But I can see you're scared and from the look of your eyes right now, I can tell that whatever it is is keeping you up at night. I want to help."

"How?" I ask, confused as to how he can help when he has no idea what haunts both my waking and sleeping hours.

"Spend the weekend with me?" My eyes widen in shock. "Let me take you away from here and everything you're worrying about."

"Joe, we can't—" All the reasons why he shouldn't even be here right now circle through my head, let alone the million and one reasons why we shouldn't spend an entire weekend together. The knowledge that I feel too connected to him already after the small amount of time we've spent together up until now is only a part of the problem.

"Forget it all. Whatever's in your head right now, forget it. I'm not a student. You're not a teacher. We're just two people enjoying their time off and each other. Let's leave all the stress behind. Just for a few days."

I can't deny that what he's proposing sounds incredible. I'm desperate to scream yes, pack a bag and drag him from the building, but I've got to think of the bigger picture here.

I sit forward on the sofa, my body willing me to get up and get ready to go, but my mind holds me back.

"What did you say to me before our night out? That you wanted to live, you wanted to experience new things. This is just like that night but longer. Let's tick a few more experiences off your list."

"What did you have in mind?"

"I've booked us a hotel in a place I think you'll love."

"You've booked it? A little presumptuous, wasn't it?"

"You're worth the risk."

My chin drops, my heart damn near stopping dead in my chest at his words. My eyes hold his as I look for any hint that he's joking, but I find nothing.

It's those four little words and the meaning behind them that has me jumping up and pulling clothes from the small wardrobe at the other side of the room and quickly stuffing everything into a holdall.

"Is that a yes?" Joe asks with a laugh as his eyes follow my every move.

"Just because you asked so politely."

"Not sure I've ever been described as polite before. Next you'll be telling me that I'm chivalrous and thoughtful." His words are quiet, like I'm not really meant to hear them. But I do.

I pause and look up. "You are."

"That's because I've only shown you that side of me."

"I don't believe that. I've seen you, Joe." He stands and my eyes drop from his to take in his body.

"So you have." He stalks over, his eyes

darkening. I see what he's doing: diverting the conversation to sex, something he's much more comfortable discussing.

I want to argue that I see more than he realises I do, but much like me not wanting to talk about my past, I can tell this is something he's not keen to discuss.

I hold his eyes when they eventually find mine once again, trying to tell him everything I want. His eyes soften, and I wonder if he understands.

"What do I need to pack? Anything special?"

"Whatever you want. You'll look gorgeous, no doubt." Flames lick at my stomach, the darkness in his eyes telling me that he's being totally sincere. Much like him, I wonder what he sees when he looks at me, because the only thing I see when I look in the mirror these days is the woman I've always wanted to be who's too afraid to really go after the life she craves.

I'm avoiding dealing with so much of my past that I've shoved it into the dark corners of my mind when the one thing that I really should be avoiding is standing right in front of me, promising me an escape.

I somehow manage to break our connection to pack my toiletries and zip up my bag.

"Did you want to finish your soup?" Joe asks, a cheeky smile curling at one side of his mouth.

"I think I'm good."

"Right answer. Come on."

Taking my bag, he throws it over one shoulder before sliding his other hand into mine. I tense, knowing that I should pull away, but touching him is just a little too comfortable. After days of looking over my shoulder, waiting for the inevitable, the feeling of safety that washes through me is too much to deny.

I squeeze his hand a little tighter, and together we lock up the flat and head down to his van.

"Doesn't your boss mind you taking the van off on a mystery weekend with a stranger?"

"First, you're not a stranger. I know you better than I know a lot of people in my life." I turn to look at him as he pushes the key into the ignition and starts the engine. There are so many words on the tip of my tongue, but I know he wants to talk about it as much as I do. So instead of asking anything, I give him a small smile when his eyes meet mine. The more time I spend with him, the more I see the shadows in his eyes he tries to cover with his confidence, but as time goes on, the darker they're getting.

It helps explain the pull I feel towards him.

We're the same, both trying to survive with plenty of skeletons hiding in our closets.

"So where are we going?"

"To the home of literature."

My brows draw together as I think about his words, but nowhere comes to mind.

"I don't—"

"I'm disappointed in you, Miss Smith," he says with a chuckle as he heads out of the city.

"I thought we were forgetting about the whole teacher/student thing?"

"We are, although where we're going should be a good field trip for me."

A thought hits me, and excitement bubbles in my belly. "Oh...we're going to Stratford-upon-Avon." I don't even ask it as a question, because the second it occurred to me, I knew I was right.

"We are. I thought we'd get up close and personal to the man himself. Although, I must admit that I'm more excited about the up close and personal opportunities with someone else." He turns to me, his teeth sinking into his bottom lip as his eyes drop to my breasts. "Did I mention how much I like that dress?"

The dress in question is a simple black jersey

wrap, cut a little lower than I'd usually risk for work, but the fabric feels incredible and I needed something a little extra to get me through today.

"Thank you," I say, my cheeks heating. I want to look away, but when his eyes lift and capture mine, I'm powerless to move.

"Do you know what's even better about it?"

I shake my head, unable to form any words.

"How incredible it'll be when I get to unwrap you from it later."

Heat races between my thighs and I shift uncomfortably, a move he doesn't miss.

"Motherfucker," Joe breathes, his chest heaving. "You're going to be the death of me."

I don't get to reply, because the car behind us at the traffic lights beeps his horn. We both look forward to see what was the green light turned back to red.

"Whoops," Joe says innocently. "He'd understand if he had you sitting beside him, distracting him."

I really doubt that.

"You act like you never get compliments, which I find hard to believe." Joe speeds up as we join the motorway, which thankfully means he's unable to look my way.

"Believe it. I think I've had more from you in the past few weeks than I have in my entire life."

His fingers wrap tighter around the wheel until his knuckles turn white, and when I glance at his body, every single muscle is pulled tight.

Reaching over, I place my hand on his forearm. "It's okay. Relax. I'm not there right now. I'm here...with you."

He blows out a breath and looks over at me quickly. His eyes show everything he's trying to hold inside. My stomach drops. If he's this angry just because of a lack of compliments, what's he going to be like when he finds out the truth?

A shudder runs through me at the thought, and I push it away. This weekend, my time with Joe isn't about any of that.

"Tell me more about you." He swallows nervously, I assume thinking that I'm going to hit him with some heavy stuff. "Okay, so...cats or dogs?"

A smile lights up his face and the skin around his eyes crinkles with amusement as he barks out a laugh.

"Easy, dogs all the way."

"Correct."

"Oh, I didn't realise this was a test, Miss Smith."

Embarrassment colours my cheeks. "Sorry, habit."

"Don't apologise." His hand sneaks over and rests high on my thigh. Its warmth and size feels too good to push away.

"Pop or hip hop?"

"Hip hop," I say without even taking a breath.

"Really?"

"All day long."

"Go on then, it's all yours." He nods towards his phone that's sitting in a clasp thing attached to the air vents.

Leaning forward, I wake it up and am greeted by his passcode screen.

"Nine seven one two," he rattles off without a second thought.

I stare at him as he focuses on where we're going.

"What?" His eyes flick to me, and I can tell he wants to hold them but he's unable to given his task at hand.

"You just gave me the code. That's like...I don't know. Serious."

"You didn't bat an eyelid about spending the weekend with me but this you freak out about?" His chuckle of amusement warms me from the inside out.

"It just seems so…"

"Serious?" he repeats. "Chill out. I can just change it later, it's not like I've given you a key to my flat or anything."

He's right, I know he is, but I also don't think I believe a word that's just fallen from his lips.

Trying to ignore the tingles racing around my body every time he glances over at me, I scroll through his music. I come to a stop when I find something that looks interesting and hit play on his 'Old Skool Trax' playlist.

He nods his head in approval and turns the volume up slightly, but not so much that we can't still hold a conversation.

"It's your turn." His hand squeezes my thigh, its heat burning my skin and making it hard to concentrate.

"Uh…night in or night out?"

"Is that a trick question?"

"No, why?"

"Wherever you are."

"That's not how this game works," I chastise,

trying to ignore the elation that bubbles up within me as I repeat his answer over and over in my head.

"You know, if you want to live a little, you've got to break the rules every now and then, right?"

"Not my forte."

"So I'm learning."

Silence falls between us, but it's not uncomfortable.

"Okay, you want a better answer? Before meeting you, night out, always a night out. The more alcohol and willing bodies the better." I sense him cringe at his own words, but it doesn't stop him. "But now, I'd willingly trade all of that for a night on your sofa."

I'm totally lost for words, and when he glances over at me, his eyes dark and hungry, it doesn't make it any better.

"Pull over or keep driving?"

"Huh, what?"

"Pull over or keep driving?" he repeats slowly. His hand creeps up a little higher on my thigh, and I gasp when his little finger grazes against my core.

Closing my eyes, I rest my head back and try to focus, to attempt to find my sanity that seems to fly out of the window whenever he's around.

"Keep driving," I whisper. It sounds unconvincing.

"Really?" His voice is deep and gravelly, and it hits exactly where he intends. My clit throbs as my body temperature increases another notch.

"Really." When I pull my eyelids open, a sign showing how close we are appears in front of me. I might be all for exploring my wild side, but I'm not sure that goes as far as getting caught for indecent exposure.

Attempting to direct the topic of conversation onto something else before I change my mind, I rack my brain for another question. The silence becomes suffocating; the only thing I'm aware of is his large, imposing body next to me and his manly scent permeating the air. I crack the window slightly despite it being bitterly cold outside.

"Marmite or peanut butter?"

"Pft, Marmite, every day of the fucking week."

"Thank god. I might have made you turn the car back if you answered that wrong."

"Salt and vinegar or cheese and onion?"

Our this and that game continues until he brings the van to a stop outside a huge Tudor building. It's exactly the kind I imagined when I figured out where we were going, and the kind of place I could only dream of staying.

"This is our hotel?" My voice is full of awe.

"Yeah. Is that okay?"

"Okay? Joe, this place is stunning. It must have cost you a damn fortune."

"As much as I'd love to agree, I actually got us an amazing last-minute deal."

"Just tell me how much my half is, and I'll make sure to pay you back."

His eyes burn into the side of my head as I bend down to grab my bag, ready to get out. A shiver runs down my spine, and when I look over at him I understand why. His eyes are full of anger and frustration. The look is one I'm familiar with, and it makes my muscles tense, ready for what's to come.

"You'll do no such thing. I booked this for you, as a gift. I don't expect anything in return." His voice is hard, but it doesn't hold the disgust or vile words I'm so used to following anger.

I open my mouth to respond, but he beats me to it.

"And don't even think about arguing."

"I wasn't," I lie. "I was going to ask if you were sure you didn't want *anything* in return."

His eyes darken further, but it's no longer with anger. They drop from mine in favour of my lips, and I can't help my tongue sneaking out to wet my bottom one in preparation for what I hope is to come. We've been together over two hours and side by side in this confined space for most of that, and he's yet to do anything aside from place his hand on my thigh and look at me like he wants to devour me.

He clears his throat. "Come on, let's check in." It takes him a few seconds to do as he suggested. His eyes are too focused on my lips to move.

Grabbing both of our bags, he takes my hand and, after placing a kiss to my knuckles, threads our fingers together and guides me towards the entrance.

"I've got a room booked for Mr. Kingsman," he says, seemingly oblivious to the girl behind the reception desk drooling over him.

"Oh um...yes. I have some good news for you as well—it seems your room has been upgraded." He looks over at me and winks. I damn near melt into a puddle on the floor.

The receptionist hands over our key and talks through a couple of things, but I don't pay any attention. I'm too busy taking note of the intricate tattoos that cover Joe's arms and hands.

"Your dinner reservation is for nine o'clock. It'll be in our restaurant just behind me," she explains seconds before Joe thanks her and takes my hand once again. "Would you like any help with your luggage?" Joe waves her off, and we head for the lift.

"I think she liked you," I say once the doors have closed us inside the small space.

"Didn't notice."

"How's that possible? She was about ready to jump the desk so she could lick you."

"You were standing next to me, Quinn. Why would I be paying attention to anyone else?"

"I...uh..." The lift opens on the top floor of the hotel, and we walk out hand in hand.

Joe holds the keycard up to the pad, and the door clicks unlocked. Dropping my hand, he reaches for the handle and pushes it open.

"After you."

I step forward and my eyes go wide.

"Wow." I walk into the huge, luxurious room, trying and failing to take it all in. The old beams are through the walls and ceilings, giving it the perfect old and rustic look that's stereotypical of the buildings here. The rest of the room is in keeping with the age of the building, but it's mixed with a few sleek modern touches.

"I was thinking the same." Having dropped the bags, Joe's hands slip around my waist and I'm pulled back against him. His heat immediately seeps into me, and I breathe a sigh of contentment.

I'm safe.

"Only, I haven't had a chance to look at the room because I can't take my eyes off you."

"Are you always this smooth?"

"Honestly?" he asks between light kisses to my neck which have my nipples pebbling behind my bra. "No. Never. I'm not ashamed to admit that I'm usually a fuck 'em and chuck 'em kind of guy."

I'm not at all surprised, but the way he says it so casually makes me wince.

"Don't go thinking that my partners were under any illusion that it was anything other than what it was. Sex. I've never wanted to spend time with someone like I do with you. I've never wanted a repeat like I do with you. I've never wanted anything from any of the people I've slept with before."

"You want something from me?" I ignore my other curiosity: that he only refers to his previous bed mates as partners or people. I pretty much figured the night I saw him dancing with and kissing anyone in touching distance that he didn't discriminate where sex was concerned. I was brought up with the idea that a woman and man meet, get married and give themselves to their spouse and their spouse only. But standing here, knowing Joe as I do, I really don't care about that part of his past.

I hope when my truth comes out, he doesn't hold it against me.

"Everything, Quinn. I want everything."

He spins me so we're face-to-face. The intensity in his eyes as he stares down at me causes my stomach to drop. *He wants things you can't offer him. Not yet, anyway.*

"Joe, I—"

"Shhh. I didn't say that to freak you out or for you to tell me you want the same from me. I just want you to know that this isn't just a bit of fun for me. How I feel about you isn't a temporary thing. I know it's complicated. I know there are a million reasons why we shouldn't be here. But we are. We're here. We're together, and I can't imagine anywhere else I want to be right now."

His lips find mine, and his tongue sweeps into

my mouth, searching for mine. Everything he's just expressed is confirmed by the way his lips move. The emotion he pours into it causes tears to burn the backs of my eyes.

What he said is everything I've ever wanted: a man who's passionate about what he wants...about me. But right now couldn't be a worse time for it.

"Fuck. I want to be inside you so badly."

"What's stopping you?"

"The fact that we've got reservations and that I've been listening to your stomach rumbling the entire journey here."

"It was not," I argue, although it's weak at best. I'm starving. If it wasn't for him and his distraction techniques, the only thing I'd be able to think about would be food.

"I might need you more than my next breath, but I also need you with a little energy. I don't plan on sleeping much tonight, so you're going to need some sustenance."

My lips form an O, and he steps away from me.

"We've got thirty minutes—not that you need it, because you look stunning already—but do what you need to do and we'll find you some food."

I'm rooted to the floor, still reeling from his kiss as he falls onto the sofa and grabs the TV remote, waking it up and finding it on a 24/7 news channel.

I don't think anything of it as I go to my bag and rummage around for something to wear.

It's not until I hear the headlines for the next story that I freeze.

"The latest private school scandal hit the headlines this morning. According to the police, there have been over one-hundred victims in contact to tell their story about abuse at Earlington Manor. The head teacher has been—"

"Turn it off." My voice is barely a whisper, making Joe turn to look at me so I can repeat my words. I do so before his eyes even find mine.

"Okay, okay. Is this okay?" he asks, turning the channel and finding a repeat of an old US sitcom.

My hands tremble, and my cold blood turns my body to ice at just hearing those words from the TV.

"Quinn?" he asks, walking over and placing his hands on my upper arms. "Are you okay? You look like you've seen a ghost."

I have, I think as memories from my past life threaten to surface.

"I'm sorry. I just can't watch that. I've worked

with too many kids who've been affected by that kind of abuse, and I can't hear any more of it."

He eyes me curiously, correctly guessing that there's a lot more to this than I'm letting on.

"I'm okay, I promise." It's a bare-faced lie and he knows it, but when I move towards the bathroom with a change of clothes and my wash bag, he allows me the space I need.

CHAPTER FOURTEEN

THE MEAL IS out of this world, and it's almost enough to drag me from my nightmare. Joe wanted to bring me here to get me away from what's haunting me, but he managed to bring it closer than it has been since the phone call from Detective Barker.

I force myself out of my own head so I can enjoy what he's done for me, but it's harder than I ever imagined it would be.

He can see it. The concern hasn't left his eyes since he released me to get ready, but thankfully he's given me the reprieve I need and not asked me about it. He wants to, he's practically vibrating with the need to, but he won't.

"Would you like coffee?" our waiter asks once she's cleared our dessert plates.

"I'm fine, but would you?" Joe's heated and concerned eyes turn to me. I ignore the concern and focus on the desire.

"No, thank you. I think I'm done." I rub my hand over my full belly. I can't remember the last time I ate an entire three-course meal. Not so long ago it would have seemed so normal, but now I live on a diet of toast and noodles, it seems like it was in another lifetime.

I swallow down the last of my wine, and Joe's eyes lock onto my lips and run down my neck as I do. His teeth sink into his bottom lip, and his muscles tense.

"I think I'm done too. I'm done with you teasing me from the other side of the table. I'm done with imagining what you're wearing under that sinful little leather dress, and I'm done waiting for another taste of your sweet pussy."

I gasp. "You can't say stuff like that here. Anyone could hear you."

"So? Anyone who's bored enough to be eavesdropping right now will only be jealous."

I glance around the full restaurant and find everyone lost in their own conversations or meals.

"Excuse me," Joe calls out when a waiter walks past. "Please could we have another bottle to take up to our room?"

"Of course, Sir. I'll be right back with it."

It feels like only seconds later that Joe has a chilled bottle of white wine in one hand and one of mine in his other.

My stomach somersaults as we step into the lift alone. The air crackles between us as Joe hits the button for the top floor and turns to me.

I back up. The look in his eyes and the tight set of his shoulders makes my heart race and my skin tingle.

He closes the distance between us and successfully sucks all the air from the tiny space. His body is impressively huge at the best of times, but right now, in such an enclosed space, he looks downright dangerous.

I feel like a little chick being hunted by its prey, but there's not an ounce of fear in my body right now.

I might be scared of many things in my life, but Joe isn't one of them. My feelings for him might be another story, but him, his strength and power, not so much.

He stops when there's barely an inch between

us. His breath races across my face. It smells like wine and chocolate from the moose he just had for dessert. It's delicious, making me desperate to know how it'll make him taste.

I expect his lips to land on mine, but much to my surprise, when we connect, it's only our foreheads that are touching.

His eyes continue to stare down into mine, and it's like he can see all the way down to my toes. The weirdest feeling comes over me, the desire to tell him everything. To spill everything I've kept so close to my chest for so long. It's right on the tip of my tongue, even though I know that now is not the time.

He makes me feel safe. He makes me feel strong. Acknowledging both of those means that I know he'll keep my secrets locked up as tightly as I do. He'll accept them and support me without question.

"Quinn," he breathes, making my insides quiver with need. "What the hell are you doing to me?"

I want to respond, to tell him that I really have no idea, but I don't get a chance because the lift doors open on our floor and we're forced to break apart.

The second the door to our fancy hotel room slams behind us, he's on me. My bag drops to the floor with a thud. I've no idea what happens to the bottle of wine, because both his hands grasp my face as his lips descend on mine. He walks us backwards until I bump up against the wall, but he doesn't stop, not until every inch of our bodies that can touch are.

His hard length presses into my stomach and he grinds his hips slowly, ensuring I feel every inch of him.

"I need you so fucking badly," he groans in my ear after kissing along my jaw. A shudder runs down my spine and radiates all the way out to my fingertips and toes. I sag against the wall as his hands skim down my sides and his fingers dig into my hips with an almost painful grip.

Something flashes in his eyes like he's made a decision, and his hands drop lower to push the fabric of my dress up around my waist.

"Fuck," he moans when he gets a look at the small black thong I'm wearing. It's a little different to the boring pair of knickers I had on the last time.

With his hands on my arse, he lifts me and presses me back against the wall. My arms wrap around his shoulders as I seek out his lips once again.

His length presses against my core, and the ball of need that's already consuming me starts to grow even more insistent. I've never experienced sex like this before. Like if we don't have each other right now and sate the desire running through us, then we might explode. I thought this kind of need and passion was something that only existed in movies and romance novels.

Joe's tongue delves deep into my mouth, exploring like he can't possibly live another second without discovering every inch.

Somehow, he manages to slip his hand between us, undo his fly and release his cock.

"Fuck, Joe," I moan when he rubs the head against the damp fabric covering me. My muscles tense and ripple, needing something to grip onto, something to fill me and give me everything I need.

"I've been tested. I'm clean. I want to feel all of you."

My head falls back against the wall with a thud. Joe's tongue licks up the column of my neck as he waits for my answer. It's not that I need to think about it...more that I need my brain to function to be able to form the correct words.

"I'm…" His tongue swirls around the outside of my ear and I lose all concentration. "I'm on the pill."

Taking that as my confirmation, the fabric of my thong is immediately pulled to the side, and he pushes himself into my wetness.

"So fucking wet for me," he murmurs, pushing the head of his cock just inside me, teasing me.

My muscles try to grip onto him to drag him deeper to get what I need. My heels dig hard into his arse, trying to get him to thrust, and he chuckles.

"What do you need, Quinn?"

"You," I moan, arching my back and shamelessly thrusting my leather covered chest at him.

"How? How do you want me?"

My cheeks heat more than they already are, knowing that he wants me to spell it out for him. But if it's what it takes to feel him pressing inside me, I'll tell him whatever he wants to hear.

"I want your cock inside me. So fucking deep my eyes cross," I add as his pupils dilate until they're almost totally black when the word 'cock' falls from my mouth.

"Gonna. Kill. Me." His words are barely loud enough for me to make out.

My lips turn up in a triumphant smile. I've never had a man at my mercy like this before, and the power it gives me makes me feel invincible.

My elation is soon pushed aside as Joe thrusts his hips, simultaneously dropping me a little lower down the wall so he fills me in one swift move.

I cry out at the sudden invasion, my body stretching almost to the point of pain to accommodate him.

"Fuuuuck," he hisses, slamming his palm down against the wall beside my head. His muscles are pulled tight, and I know he's trying to give me a minute to adjust, but he's dying to move.

Moving my head from the wall, I let my lips brush his ear. "Fuck me, Joe. Fuck me until the only thing I can think about is you. Make everything else go away."

"Motherfucking shit. Where have you been all my life?"

I assume it's a rhetorical question. His fingers tangle in my hair and my head's pulled back so he can slam his lips down on mine.

His hips find their rhythm and, before long,

we're forced to break our kiss so we can both suck in some much-needed air.

My head hits the wall, but if it hurts I don't feel it. The only thing I can focus on is the building tension radiating from my core that's sure to rock my world when it explodes.

"So tight. So wet. So fucking good," Joe chants against the hot skin of my neck as he ups the pace, chasing both of our releases. "Fuck, Quinn. Fuuuuuuck," he roars so loud that I've no doubt the rooms either side of us heard, but I don't care. All I care about is the twitch of his cock inside me and the hot spurts of his cum that set off my own mind-blowing release. My muscles clamp down around him as fireworks shoot off around me. My body takes on a life of its own as it twitches and convulses, the pleasure he's caused seemingly endless and so fucking needed.

Our chests are heaving and our skin's covered in a sheen of sweat when Joe pulls out of me and drops my legs to the floor.

"Turn," he demands.

It takes a few seconds for me to figure out if my legs will hold me up before I follow his orders. My knees threaten to buckle the moment I move them, but thankfully, I don't crumple to a pile on the floor.

The second my back is to him, his fingers grip onto the zip at the base of my neck and he pulls it down. My breasts swell once again, my nipples puckering against the lace containing them.

Goosebumps break out across my skin when he pushes the fabric from my shoulders.

"It feels like it's been a lifetime since I've touched you." He kisses down my spine until he finds the clasp of my bra. He unhooks it and allows it to fall to the floor.

Descending, he pulls my thong down my legs before helping me slip my shoes from my feet.

"Turn," he repeats.

After sucking in some confidence, I spin. My skin heats under his intense stare, my nipples harden even further, and my core grows hot for him once again.

Reaching behind his head, he pulls his shirt from his body, revealing his rippling muscles beneath before pushing his jeans and boxers from his hips and toeing off his shoes.

I take my time running my eyes over every inch of him, but my ogling is soon stopped when I'm pulled into his arms and thrown onto the bed.

"I hope you didn't think we were done."

"Not even for a second. Sleep is for the weak, right?" He laughs, and it awakens something inside me that I didn't even realise was missing until right now. My heart swells seeing the wide, genuine smile on his handsome face. I want to wrap my arms around him and never let go, and that's a seriously scary thought. I've never wanted anything as much as I want him, and I already know that nothing good can come from being with me.

I'VE no idea what time we eventually fall asleep, but when I wake it's with Joe's arms locked around me. I breathe a sigh of relief when I realise that I had my first peaceful night's sleep (even if it was only a few hours) since he was with me last time. I put it down to my exhaustion, but I can't help hoping it's more than that, because for the first time in weeks, I feel safe. While I'm in his arms, I know nothing's going to happen to me.

Needing to see him, I try to turn in his arms without waking him. I barely move and my muscles pull, a reminder of just how busy we got last night. I'm most definitely not used to that kind of exertion.

His breathing stays steady and he doesn't move so I think I'm successful, but when I look up, I find him staring back down at me, his eyes full of amusement.

"Hey," I say shyly, suddenly very aware of the fact my naked body is crushed up against his.

"Hi." Something wicked twinkles in his eyes, and my stomach tumbles in anticipation of what's to come. "You hungry?"

"Uh...I guess. What time is breakfast?"

"Right now." Before I have a chance to blink, he's thrown the covers off and is trailing a line of kisses down my stomach.

My body immediately wakes up for him, and my veins fill with fire, knowing what he's about to do to me.

It's safe to say I've never had an alarm clock like this before and I'm pretty sure I'd quite happily keep it. The serious thought makes me still for a beat, and he doesn't miss it. He's hovering over my navel when he looks up and his eyes find mine. He doesn't say any words, but I can feel the question in his stare. Forcing a small smile onto my lips, I nod slightly. He holds our connection for a second longer, I guess trying to figure out if I really am okay or not, but before long the soft brush of his lips under my belly button has goosebumps pricking my skin.

"So fucking sweet. I could eat you all day long, Quinn." Heat floods my face at the thought.

"You won't hear me complaining." I'm not sure how I've managed my entire life without this but after just one lick from his skilled tongue and I feel myself becoming addicted to his touch.

His tongue sweeps up the length of me, making my back arch. Needing more of what he's got to give, I thread my fingers into his hair and hold him down. His chuckle only adds to the sensations he's causing.

Sooner than I was expecting, with two fingers deep inside me and his tongue circling my clit, I come all over his face. He doesn't stop until the last tremors of my orgasm have subsided. When he sits up, it's with the smuggest smile playing on his lips.

"Pleased with yourself?" I ask with a laugh.

He crawls over me, holds my face in his hand and stares deep into my eyes. "You just screamed my name over and over. Of course I'm fucking pleased with myself."

I go to laugh, but his lips cover mine. I hesitate

because...morning breath, but it doesn't seem to bother Joe as he slips his tongue inside my mouth. I eagerly return his kiss, the fire he'd doused inside me sparking back to life the second I taste myself on him.

Without breaking our kiss, he situates himself at my entrance, and we both sigh when he slowly slides inside me.

Last night we fucked, and we fucked hard. Hence my aching muscles this morning. But this, this is something totally different. It's slower, it's more...sensual, and when he pulls back and looks into my eyes, I can't help but feel like he's trying to tell me something. Something I'm nowhere near ready to accept or deal with. Tears sting my eyes, and I fight to keep them down, but when he drops his forehead against mine, his hand splayed across my throat possessively, I can't prevent one escaping.

His eyes darken the moment he sees it, and he lifts his hand so he can wipe it away.

"Fuck, Quinn." He doesn't say anything else. He doesn't need to. His eyes say it all as he searches mine, I fear trying to find the same things that he's feeling right now.

I've no idea if he finds what he's looking for,

but after a second or two, he drops his lips back to mine and kisses me until we find our simultaneous releases. It's different to the previous ones he's given me. It's calmer, slower, but by no means any less earth-shattering.

"Come on, let's shower." He gets up and walks to the bathroom. My heart drops when I see the slight slump to his shoulders. Did I just disappoint him somehow?

He washes me thoroughly, but although he's attentive, I still can't help but feel like he's suddenly holding back. I want to ask, I'm desperate to, but I'm also aware that asking him too many questions will probably come with consequences: him asking some of his own. The thought of trying to explain everything has my heart racing in panic.

"HAVE YOU BEEN HERE BEFORE?" he asks when we step from the hotel hand-in-hand with bellies full of an incredible fried breakfast and fresh fruit.

"Yeah, I think I came here on a school trip years ago, but I hardly remember it. You?"

"No, never. I'm a Londoner through and through."

"You've never left?"

"Of course. I had holidays and stuff as a kid, but they were always abroad."

"That must have been nice," I say, thinking that I'd have loved to get out of our little town and experience some of the world.

"Yes and no."

"Oh?"

"Pass," he says. His hand tightens in mine, and I feel him physically shut down. I hate it, but at the same time part of me feels glad that I'm not the only one holding back. I feel less guilty about hiding my past from my possible future. *My future,* is that what this is?

We have an incredible morning visiting all the sights—Shakespeare's home and his wife's childhood home, along with others that are connected to his life.

The history is incredible, and I find myself picturing what it must have been like for him back then, writing such epic literature in such a stunning place. I don't have a creative bone in my body, but even I feel inspired being here.

We stop in a café for a light lunch before

heading for the Church of the Holy Trinity. The building is out of this world. Its age, its history, everything about it just blows me away, and I'm not ashamed to admit that it drags a little emotion up into my throat as I stand and stare.

"Are you okay?" Joe whispers in my ear when he notices the tears threatening to spill from my eyes.

"Yeah. I'm good."

"Do you want to just sit for a bit?"

Nodding, I make my way over to the closest pew and slide along a little so he can sit beside me.

He's silent, allowing me the time I need to deal with my thoughts. I stare ahead at the chancel, taking in the ornate carved wood and the huge stones that make up the building. Suddenly, without realising, words start tumbling from my mouth.

"I'm married." Joe gasps beside me, but otherwise he does nothing other than to continue staring ahead and allow me to speak. "I was promised to him from as early as I can remember. I know that sounds incredibly old fashioned, but my parents were—are—really traditional. There was never any other option for me despite what I really wanted. I had no choice. I went along with the wedding, telling myself that I'd learn to like him, love him even, but it was never meant to be.

"I was terrified of disappointing my father. He...he has a terrible temper, and I could only imagine what my refusal would result in, so I toed the line, kept their secrets and swept their indiscretions under the carpet like I'd watched my mother do all my life. It was normal. It was my life. We lived in this little bubble, and the days just passed while I dreamt of other things.

"I knew from the get go that we weren't a match made in heaven, but there was no way I could shame my parents and leave. But then..." I trail off, not wanting to go into details of the reason I couldn't deal with it all anymore.

Joe blows out a long breath, and I find myself releasing the air I didn't know I was holding. I immediately feel lighter for confessing just a small part of the secret I'm forced to live with.

"My parents disowned me when I was fifteen, after they found out I was bi." His words are flat, cold, and my heart aches for the little boy that's clearly still so hurt by that.

"Arseholes," I mutter, not meaning for the word to come out aloud.

"I couldn't agree more. I mean, I'll be the first

to admit that I was an awful teenager, but I didn't mean to make their lives hard. Well...not in the beginning. I was just trying to figure out who I was and where I fit in the world. Then they discovered me and the boy next door at the bottom of our garden, and I became and even bigger threat to their perfect life. The only way to stop me 'ruining everything' was to get rid of me."

We both sit in silence, the words we just said hanging heavy in the small space between us. The last few minutes might have been intense, but I feel better than I have in a long time.

I don't need to see his head turning to know he's looking at me, his intense stare burns into the side of my face.

Closing my eyes for a beat, I turn to look at him. His face is expressionless aside from his dark, haunted eyes.

"Thank you, for telling me. For trusting me."

"I do trust you, Joe. I just...it's hard for me to go back there."

"I get it. Take all the time you need."

"I hope you realise your parents missed out with the choice they made. They should be so proud of you."

He shrugs. "I'm not so sure about that, I've

done some pretty fucked up shit over the years. I probably shouldn't even be allowed in a church." He glances around, and I can't help but laugh at the expression on his face.

"Everyone makes mistakes. It helps shape who we are."

"Do you think that when you think of *him?*" The disdain in his voice is clear, and it almost makes me regret telling him.

"I'm not sure he shaped me all that much aside from showing me exactly what I didn't want."

"You've only told me part of the story, Quinn, but I already know that you're one of the strongest women I know."

I shrug and look away. I don't see myself that way. As far as I'm concerned, I'm weak. Weak for living someone else's life for so long, weak for not following my own dreams, and weak for not exposing those around me for who they really were. But I don't voice any of that for fear of what he might say.

"Shall we move before this gets any heavier?" I ask, hoping for a reprieve from the seriousness of our lives.

"Sounds good."

Joe slides from the wooden pew and holds out

his hand for me. I don't hesitate in placing mine in his.

Once I'm standing, he leans down and whispers in my ear. "Thank you for not freaking out."

I glance up at him, wondering if the truth about his life has been haunting him as much as my own has been.

"You can tell me anything. I won't judge. Our pasts are our pasts. I'd much rather spend my time looking forward than back."

CHAPTER FIFTEEN

I SWEAR I blink and our weekend together is over. Nothing more is said about our confessions in the church, and I couldn't be more grateful. I'm glad I did it. I wanted to show to Joe that I was trying to let him in, just like he was me, but that doesn't mean I'm ready to spill any more yet. The time is coming. I can only avoid it and the media for so long. With every minute that ticks around, I know I'm a minute closer to another phone call from Detective Barker and reliving my old life in front of a judge. As much as I want justice for the people they've hurt, I also can't imagine explaining what monsters they are to their faces. They're men I should love, men I should try to protect. Not testify against.

A shudder runs down my spine, and I pause my packing.

Joe's hands land on my hips, and he pulls me back into him. His lips trail up my neck until he nibbles around my ear. "I'm not ready to leave this room." He doesn't need to say the words, the feeling of his erection digging into my arse tells me everything I need to know.

"Me neither." My head rolls to the side as his kisses continue. He parts his lips and his tongue sweeps across my skin. My heart pounds and my temperature soars, despite only having a Joe-induced orgasm less than thirty minutes ago in the shower.

The atmosphere is heavy as Joe drags both our bags from the bed and we walk out of our little sanctuary.

I let out a giant sigh as the hotel room door clicks shut behind us. Joe squeezes my hand a little tighter in support.

We check out, find his van, and almost before I've had time to think we're on our way back towards the city.

"So your boss doesn't mind you taking your work van away for the weekend?" I ask again, seeing as I didn't get an answer when I asked yesterday.

"I sure hope not, because I didn't exactly ask," he says with a laugh. "I'm sure it'll be fine, my boss is banging my best friend. She can help me make him see things from my perspective." He visibly cringes as the words pass his lips.

"Tell me about her?"

"Who? Lauren?"

"Yeah."

"She's..." he sighs, a small smile playing on his lips as he thinks of her. "She's incredible. One of the strongest women I know, and not just because she's put up with my shit all these years. We met at a pretty low point in both of our lives, almost like fate. She's been my rock."

"She really means a lot to you, doesn't she?" I don't know why I ask; it's obvious from his tone how important she is to him.

"You've no idea."

A weird feeling twists my insides. Is that...is that jealousy? The more I try not to think about it, the more it starts to fester.

"Have you known each other long?"

"Six years or so. I turned up at the office of the

company I work for and she was there, the boss'
daughter."

"I thought she was banging the boss?"

"Long story, but her dad passed away and Ben
took over. They now live together, and I'm waiting
for a proposal to happen any moment now. What
about you, did you leave a best friend behind?"

Sadness washes over me as reality hits me once
again. "No. Eddie is actually the closest thing I've
had to a real friend in a very long time."

"Eddie?" he asks, his brows drawn together
when he glances over at me.

"Yeah. Mr. Boring."

"Oh, him. I wouldn't have put you two together."

"He's a good guy. He set me up with my flat
and got me the job. I just have to look past the fact
that he's from my previous life and knows things
about me that I'd rather no one did."

"Even me?"

I blow out a long, slow breath. "I'll tell you
everything, just...just not all at once."

Reaching across the centre console, he takes
my hand in his, his thumb rubbing the inside of my
wrist. It's a move I've never felt before, and it's
more comforting than I want to admit.

The van falls into silence, but it's not uncomfortable. I run the events of the past couple of days around my head in order to keep my past out, and I can't help but wish it was Friday night again and that we were driving in the opposite direction.

We're in the city long before I'm ready, and even sooner Joe is pulling up into my building's car park.

We both remain seated. The only sounds in the van are that of our deep breathing. I don't want to get out and, from the tense set of his body, I don't think he wants to allow me to leave either.

The moment I step out of this car, reality is going to come crashing back down on me. Tomorrow is the start of a new week. I've got to walk into college with my head held high like I haven't spent the weekend with one of my students. I've got to pretend that I'm not as bad as the people I left behind. That thought has my heart racing.

I'm not one of them.

I'm nothing like them.

This is...this is more than the nightmares and ruined childhoods they caused.

"Quinn, it's okay." Joe's warm palm gently

touches my cheek and encourages me to turn towards him.

"We shouldn't be doing this, Joe. It's wrong."

"Nothing, and I mean nothing, about this feels wrong." His thumb brushes over my bottom lip. "If it's too much, just tell me and I'll quit. I'll see if I can find a course somewhere else or something, but I'm not allowing it to come between us."

"You can't do that. This is your dream, your future."

"Bettering myself and improving my career is only part of my future. Right now, there's something else I need more."

His words hang heavy between us. I desperately want to agree and allow myself to see where this thing between us might go, but I'm scared. Terrified actually.

"Joe, I—"

"Let's not do this now. Let me walk you up?"

I should say no, but when I open my mouth, those aren't the words that fall out. "Sure."

By the time I pull myself from the passenger seat, Joe is already walking towards me, having retrieved my bag from the back of his van.

"If you're lucky, I'll give you a little something to tide you over until after work tomorrow."

Ignoring the heat that rushes through my body, I turn to look up at him. "I don't remember agreeing to seeing you tomorrow night."

"I wasn't aware I needed your permission."

I want to argue, but the sight of the front door of my building makes me lose focus. The panels where the glass used to be is now two panels of plywood, and the metal by the lock is very obviously buckled.

My heart jumps into my throat, and my stomach turns over. I don't need any more information to know who it was that caused that.

I can feel it.

As I go to take a step forward, I swear my fucking bones tremble with fear.

Will he be upstairs waiting for me? Was my paranoia warranted? Have I been being followed?

A million and one thoughts and fears hit me at once as I fight to drag in the breath I desperately need while not trying to look like a total head case in front of Joe.

"What the fuck is wrong with people?" he asks, walking us up to the door and giving it no more than a gentle shove to make it open. "Fucking kids."

If I were a little more focused on him right

now, I might make a joke about the kind of teenager he was, because from the things he's hinted at this weekend, breaking into a flat building is probably tame for what he got up to.

"They probably just wanted to steal the post or something," I mutter, not believing a word of it. "I'm okay from here if you want to head off home."

"I thought I just promised you another orgasm."

"I know, but I've already taken up all of your weekend. I'm sure you've got better things to be doing."

"Absolutely not. Trust me when I say that there's nowhere I'd rather be, or anything else I'd rather be doing right now than be with you."

I nod but I don't really register the words. I know I should be swooning, but I'm too focused on what I'm going to find on the other side of the door.

"I know what you're trying to do, Quinn, and it won't work."

"What's that?" I ask, feigning innocence.

"You're trying to hide the fact that you're scared by pushing me away."

Damn him.

"I...I..." Sucking in a deep breath, I allow the

fear I'm trying to stamp down to rumble down my spine.

"What are you scared of?"

"I'm just being silly. Come on, I'm sure it's just a broken door."

He looks at me curiously, but after pausing for a beat he gestures for me to walk into the building.

Everything looks as it usually does as we climb the stairs. The terrible graffiti is still covering the walls. The same bare patches on the steps stare up at me. Every single thing is exactly the same as every other time I've been here, until we're facing my door.

"Fuck," Joe barks, but I'm frozen in fear at the sight of my door ajar.

He was here.

This isn't some kind of shitty luck that they chose my empty flat to break into. This has been planned. Planned to ensure I'm terrified in the hope that I'll bend to his wishes to retract everything I'd accused him of.

Not happening.

My body rattles with fear, but I refuse to allow him to continue to ruin my life. I muster up some strength from somewhere and take a step forward.

"Quinn, wait."

I ignore Joe's call and push my door open.

Everything looks exactly as I left it.

My only item worth any money, my laptop, is still sitting on the coffee table where I put it after work on Friday night.

"What the hell?" Joe asks, stepping into the flat and casting his eyes around the room.

"Maybe they got scared off after they broke in," I offer as an explanation. He nods, accepting it as a possibility, but I know better.

This wasn't kids, and no one was scared off.

This is a warning.

My stomach turns, bile burning up my throat as I think about him being here. In the one safe place I've got.

"Come home with me tonight."

"What?" I ask, not registering the words he's saying as I stand frozen in the middle of my living room.

"Come home with me. We'll sort out a locksmith from there."

"No, I—"

"No arguing. I'm not leaving you here." His eyes scan over my face, and I hate to think of the terrified girl he probably sees. "Grab what you need for work tomorrow."

I stare at him for a second or two. I desperately want to argue, but when his eyebrow twitches in a 'don't start with me' gesture, I swallow down the words and turn towards the bathroom.

Stepping into the room, I go to gather up a few bits that I didn't take with me this weekend, but I'm frozen in my tracks.

I try not to react, but I can't stop a scream from passing my lips at the sight.

"Quinn?"

"Sorry, spider," I shout back, pushing the door closed so he can't look into the room.

I stare at the mirror hanging over the basin and fight to keep the contents of my stomach where they should be.

*I'm watching you...*is scrawled across the glass in red lipstick. The arsehole's even finished it off with a little kiss.

My fists clench until my nails begin to cut into my skin.

The longer I stare at the words, the more my anger starts to bubble up within me. How dare he? How fucking dare he force his way into my new life in an attempt to scare me?

Racing forward, I grab a packet of face wipes

that are sitting on the counter, pull a few out and start scrubbing.

I need him gone. Out of my life and out of my head. I've already spent enough years being controlled by him. I refuse to allow him to continue to do so.

Suddenly, the thought of the court case that's to come doesn't seem so daunting. This man needs putting behind bars—he has done for a long time. How he's allowed to roam the streets after all the evidence that's piling up against him is beyond me.

"Are you okay?" Joe's concerned voice fills the small room and something inside me immediately settles. I need to tell him everything. If that monster's after me, then I need him to know the truth.

"Yeah, just coming." I double-check the mirror to ensure there's no evidence left behind before pulling the door open and stepping from the room.

THE RIDE to Joe's place is in silence. I might have tried convincing him that that was just an everyday burglary, but I'm pretty sure I'm not fooling him. The way his fingers grip the wheel and the hard set of his jaw tells me he's more than suspicious, and I'm incredibly grateful he's managed to hold off the questions. For now at least.

He pulls up outside a pretty standard looking apartment building and drags our stuff from the back before guiding me towards the entrance.

There's an out of order sign on the lift as we pass in favour of the stairs, and I follow him up to the third floor. This place isn't flashy by any stretch of the imagination, but it's a hell of a lot better than the building I live in. There's no graffiti over the walls, the paint looks relatively fresh, and the flooring isn't chipped and fading.

"Come on, we should have the place to ourselves."

"Oh, you don't live alone?"

"No, this is my friend's place. I'm currently crashing in her spare room, but she's met someone and will be out with him."

"Okay." I nod and follow him into the flat. If he didn't tell me a woman lived here, then it would be instantly obvious. There are candles, cushions, and little girly trinkets everywhere. It's cute, exactly how I'd want my home to look if I actually had one and a little money

I jump a mile when Joe drops the bags to the

floor with a bang. I thought I'd managed to put what happened at my place behind me on the drive over, but it seems I might just be lying to myself.

"Fuck." His eyes run the length of me, and for a second I fear he's going to send me away. But when they return to mine a few shades darker, I realise it's not with fear but something else entirely.

He takes a step forward. His hand glides across my jaw and his fingers thread in my hair so he can tilt my head to just the right angle for him to slam his lips on mine and plunge his tongue between.

His kiss is exactly what I need to forget. I lift my arms around his neck at the same time he lifts me and presses me back against the wall.

All thoughts of the man inside my flat this weekend leave as he kisses me like he might die without it.

I moan with desire as he trails his lips across my jaw and begins sucking on the sensitive skin below my ear.

"Let me make you forget."

"Yes."

"Let me make you feel safe."

A noise rumbles up my throat, and when it erupts, I can only describe it as a needy purr.

Whatever it is, it makes Joe smile against my throat, his weekend long scruff scratching at my sensitive skin and sending shivers down my spine.

His fingers make quick work of unzipping my coat before his palms cup my heavy, needy breasts. My head falls back and he makes the most of my exposed neck. As good as his hands feel, I need them on my skin.

"More, Joe. More."

He pulls back and his eyes are wild with desire. "I'll give you everything, Quinn." His eyes lock onto mine, and the intensity and honesty within them make me want to look away, to break our connection, but it's too strong. All I can do is stare back, hoping like hell he's not going to break me even worse than my past tried to.

He's totally lost one second and then seems to remember exactly what he's meant to be doing the next.

My skirt is pushed up around my waist, and my boot covered legs loosen around him so he can slip his hand between us.

Like an expert, he pops the button on his jeans and pushes them and his boxers down his thighs before pulling the lace of my knickers aside.

The head of his cock nudges against my

entrance. I expect him to push straight inside, but instead I find him leaning forward so he can whisper in my ear. "I don't have all that much to give you. But this," he surges forward, making me gasp, "this I can give you until my last breath."

It's his admission and the uncertainty in his words that make my heart tumble. He pulls back slightly, his hands on my arse squeezing almost painfully. His eyes find mine once again, and I find everything he's not saying staring right back at me. My chest constricts and I'm under no illusion that right there, in the hallway of his flat, is the moment I surrender to exactly how I feel about this bad boy nerd.

"Joe, I—" I start, feeling compelled to attempt to tell him how I feel, but my words are cut off by his lips.

"Just feel," he whispers against me.

I do as I'm told.

My head falls back against the wall, and I focus on where we're connected. Sparks shoot off around my body as he pulls almost all the way back out of me.

"Please, please," I chant, needing to feel him filling me and stretching me once again.

My begging must snap his restraint, because he

lets me slide down the wall slightly, allowing him to hit me even deeper when he thrusts.

He grunts when he slams deep inside me but doesn't stop this time. He pounds into me over and over, and I can't get enough.

My thighs tremble around him, my skin flushes, and the tightening of my centre tells me that I'm about to explode. My fingernails dig into his clothed shoulders as I prepare for what's about to hit me when the atmosphere around me shifts.

What the...? Dragging my eyes open, I have to blink a few times before the two figures standing, gawping at us come into focus. Embarassment hits me, knowing we've been caught. I'm mortified to be found in such a position, especially after having to keep what's been growing between us a secret for so long.

"Fuck. I thought you said it would be safe," I whisper, my voice quivering as I try to hold it together while looking at their shocked faces. The guy casts his eyes aside, clearly giving us the privacy we deserve, whereas the woman is looking between the two of us like we're the most fascinating thing she's ever seen.

"I didn't think...fuck. Some privacy?" Joe's eyes don't leave me. I can feel his stare burning into the side of my face as he talks. It's does nothing to quash my embarassment.

"Yeah, shit. Sorry. Let's go to your place," the woman, who I can only assume is Joe's flatmate, says, wrapping her hand around the man beside her's forearm and slowly backing towards the door. At the last minute, Joe turns to look at her and some weird silent conversation passes between them.

Silence hangs heavy between us long after the door bangs shut.

"I'm sorry. I'm so fucking sorry. I didn't think..." he trails off.

"It's okay," I lie. In reality, it's anything but fine. Being caught with my legs wrapped around one of my students was the reality check I really didn't want.

"We shouldn't be doing this, Joe. This is wrong."

He doesn't want to, but when I tense my legs he releases his hold on me. Once I'm on my feet, I pull my dress back down tend start pacing.

My life is already one big disaster, and here I am allowing one of my students—okay, an adult student, although I'm sure that won't make much difference in the eyes of my boss—to fuck me against the wall. I need my job. It's the only thing I've got.

"I need...I need...fuck." Just the thought of telling him that this is over threatens to tear my heart in two. It's only made worse when I look up and take in the devastated expression on his face.

"Don't do this, Quinn. Please, don't do this. Erica's one of my best friends, she won't have an issue."

"It's not about her, Joe. I'm sure she's lovely and only wants the best for you but...this is my life. My career is my life, that's all I have right now, and I can't risk losing it for something..."

"For something what, Quinn? This isn't some big game we're playing here. I'm serious about this...about you. And I can say with total honesty that I've never said that to another person in my life. I won't allow what we have here to ruin your career."

"How? How can you stand there and promise me that? I'm breaking the one rule I always said I'd never touch. It's goes against everything I've ever...fuck," I shout, dropping my head into my hands. *You're just as bad as them,* a little voice sings in my ear. "No, no, no."

I lose myself in my panic. I've no idea how long

I stand there chanting, trying to convince myself that I'm different, that this is different, but when I come back to myself I'm wrapped in Joe's strong arms.

"It's okay, babe."

"I should leave." My voice is weak and pathetic, and I hate it.

"I'm not allowing you out of here until I know a locksmith has sorted your door out. I need to know you're safe when I'm not with you." I want to tell him that I'm not safe full stop while my past is lurking, but I keep my lips shut.

"Stay with me tonight. Let me order us dinner and you can sleep here. Tomorrow I'll get a locksmith and extra security added to your door, and then if you need some space," he says through gritted teeth, the muscle in his jaw twitching ferociously, "you can take what you need and I'll be able to sleep, knowing you're safe."

I want to argue, but what he's proposing is too tempting. I should walk out of his front door and not look back but...I can't.

"Okay," I whisper, and his arms tighten around me.

OUR NIGHT together is quiet at best. Joe allows me the space I need to try to process everything, but I fear no amount of time is going to help me figure this out. I want him. I want him like I've never wanted anything in my life, but is it enough to give up on the only thing I've got left? The only thing I've ever really had? He keeps saying that he'll quit, but I can't allow that. He deserves this second chance at his education. He deserves to follow his dreams. It's just all so fucked up, and what I'm running from doesn't even feature. When *he* shows his face again, and I know he will if he's gone to the effort of finding me, then shit's really going to hit the fan.

We don't finish what we started earlier against the wall. Joe doesn't even attempt it. Instead, when we fall into his bed, he just pulls me close and falls asleep with his arm locked around my waist and his cock snugly pressed against my arse.

I lie there all night, trying to make sense of everything, but by the time daylight starts to show through the gap in the curtains, I'm no closer to making any kind of decision.

There's a heavy tension between us as we both get ready for work. Joe knows what's coming, and I can't help but think he's trying to put off the inevitable, hoping that I'll have forgotten. Sadly, that's nowhere near the case.

"Can I drop you off?"

"Around the corner, yeah."

I follow him down to his van, emotion clogging my throat, knowing that our time is passing me by too quickly, but I know I'm doing the right thing.

Neither of us says anything as Joe fights with the rush hour traffic to get me to college, and when we pull up at the curb around the back of the building, we both let out heavy sighs.

"When can I see you again?"

"You'll be in class Thursday, right?"

"Let me quit. I'll re-enroll somewhere else. Please, Quinn. It doesn't need to be like this."

"Just give me a few days. This weekend has been...intense. I'll see you Thursday, and we'll talk after."

"Promise?"

"Promise."

I walk away with a heavy heart. I want the promise I made to be true, but really I've no idea. My head's a mess, and as I walk away with his stare making my spine tingle, I fight the need to turn and run back into his arms.

The day drags. Jodi looks like she's not slept or

eaten all weekend, although I don't spot any more bruises. I'm not stupid enough to believe that they're not hiding below her clothes. I know she's been in for a meeting, but she doesn't say anything or give away that she clearly must know it was me who reported it.

It's just after lunchtime when Eddie knocks on my classroom door and walks inside with something in his hand.

"Did you have a good weekend?" he asks curiously when he reaches my desk.

Thoughts of my weekend has tears burning the back of my throat. "Y-yeah, thank you. You?"

"Same old, same old. Here, these were just dropped off for you." His eyebrow lifts as he hands me a set of keys.

"My flat was broken into. I've had all the locks redone." *Or Joe has.* I try to ignore the feelings that threaten to bubble up, knowing that he's sorted all of this for me today.

"Oh shit. Everything seemed normal when I popped around on Saturday afternoon. Was anything stolen?"

"Not that I could see, but I didn't stay there long after I discovered it." I ignore the fact that he was there, hoping he doesn't ask where I was.

"Where did you go if you didn't stay?"

"Oh...uh...a friend's." I say it with a wince, because Eddie knows full well that he's my only friend.

His face hardens. "You know I'm only at the end of the phone if you need anything." There's something different in his tone, and I fear he's already more suspicious about what I'm up to than he should be.

"I do, thank you."

Thankfully, one of my students puts their hand up to ask a question and our conversation comes to an end before he shows himself out. The last thing I need is Eddie poking his nose in any more and discovering what I've really been doing. He found me this job when I needed it the most; I'm sure he could take it away from me just as quickly. He likes to make out that he's my friend, but a huge part of him isn't all that different from those I left behind. His reputation is more important than a lot of other things I'd consider much more important. I can only imagine how he'd feel if I were to bring scandal down on his department after he grovelled to employ me.

I'm a nervous wreck as I make the short walk from the tube station to my building later that night. It's dark and raining too heavily for the fact that I don't have an umbrella or even a hood on my coat. Water is running down my face by the time I get to the still broken front door. I guess that wasn't really for Joe to get involved with.

My heart's in my throat as I climb the stairs.

It'll be fine. I've got new locks. He can't hurt me.

I've got my new keys clasped so tightly in my hand that the metal is cutting into my skin, but I don't register the pain as my eyes dart around to see if anything is untoward.

I come to a stop in front of my door, relaxing a little when I see the two new locks. My hand trembles as I lift it to slide the key in and find out which key is for which.

I just get the key in the second lock and am about to push the door open when a squeak sounds out from behind me.

My body tenses and my spine straightens, but I don't get a chance to turn.

"Good evening, Elizabeth. You wouldn't believe how much I've missed my wife."

My mouth opens, ready to scream, but it's too late because his hand comes down on my mouth, successfully cutting off any chance I had of getting anyone's attention.

He pushes the door open and then forces me through before slamming it behind us and cutting me off from the rest of the world.

"Oh, princess. We're going to have so much fun."

A blinding pain to my head is the last thing I remember before I'm sucked into a blissfully silent darkness.

Are you ready for more? The conclusion to Quinn and Joe's story is out now!
DOWNLOAD NOW

ACKNOWLEDGMENTS

I've been looking forward to finding out a little more about Joe since I first introduced him in *Losing the Forbidden*. His story has been a long time coming, and for a while it was really up in the air as to who he was going to fall for, but the moment I realised that he craved something more from his life there was only one woman for the job. A woman who possibly has more secrets and a past she wants to keep hidden even more than Joe does.

I hope you've enjoyed the first part of Joe and Quinn's story. There is still so much more to discover about these two before they get the chance at a happily-ever-after.

This series is very quickly coming to an end, but don't worry, I've already got plans for what's coming next. All will be revealed in the next book (I hope!).

As always, I have so many people to thank. My long-suffering beta readers who have been waiting for Joe's story for what must feel like forever,

Deanna, Lindsay, Suzanne and Tracy, thank you so much for dropping everything to find out a few of Joe's secrets.

A huge thank you to Samantha for helping make my life so much easier and keeping me in check and organised. I'm seriously not sure how I ever coped without you.

Eyelyn, as always, thank you for believing in my characters and helping me make them as good as they can be.

Paige, for being the final set of eyes and polishing everything up at the last minute.

And last but not least, all my readers for supporting me on this crazy journey and for loving my characters as much as I do.

Until next time,

Tracy xo

ABOUT THE AUTHOR

Tracy Lorraine is a *USA Today* and *Wall Street Journal* bestselling new adult and contemporary romance author. Tracy has recently turned thirty and lives in a cute Cotswold village in England with her husband, baby girl and lovable but slightly crazy dog. Having always been a bookaholic with her head stuck in her Kindle, Tracy decided to try her hand at a story idea she dreamt up and hasn't looked back since.

Be the first to find out about new releases and offers. Sign up to my newsletter here.

If you want to know what I'm up to and see teasers and snippets of what I'm working on, then you need to be in my Facebook group. Join Tracy's Angels here.

Keep up to date with Tracy's books at
www.tracylorraine.com

ALSO BY TRACY LORRAINE

Falling Series

Falling for Ryan: Part One #1

Falling for Ryan: Part Two #2

Falling for Jax #3

Falling for Daniel (A Falling Series Novella)

Falling for Ruben #4

Falling for Fin #5

Falling for Lucas #6

Falling for Caleb #7

Falling for Declan #8

Falling For Liam #9

Forbidden Series

Falling for the Forbidden #1

Losing the Forbidden #2

Fighting for the Forbidden #3

Craving Redemption #4

Demanding Redemption #5

<u>Avoiding Temptation</u> #6

<u>Chasing Temptation</u> #7

<u>Rebel Ink Series</u>

<u>Hate You</u> #1

<u>Trick You</u> #2

<u>Defy You</u> #3

<u>Play You</u> #4

<u>Inked</u> (A Rebel Ink/Driven Crossover)

<u>Rosewood High Series</u>

<u>Thorn</u> #1

<u>Paine</u> #2

<u>Savage</u> #3

<u>Fierce</u> #4

<u>Hunter</u> #5

Faze (#6 Prequel)

<u>Fury</u> #6

<u>Legend</u> #7

<u>Maddison Kings University Series</u>

<u>TMYM: Prequel</u>

TRYS #1

TDYW #2

TBYS #3

TVYC #4

TDYD #5

TDYR #6

TRYD #7

Knight's Ridge Empire Series

Wicked Summer Knight: Prequel (Stella & Seb)

Wicked Knight #1 (Stella & Seb)

Wicked Princess #2 (Stella & Seb)

Wicked Empire #3 (Stella & Seb)

Deviant Knight #4 (Emmie & Theo)

Deviant Princess #5 (Emmie & Theo

Deviant Reign #6 (Emmie & Theo)

One Reckless Knight (Jodie & Toby)

Reckless Knight #7 (Jodie & Toby)

Reckless Princess #8 (Jodie & Toby)

Reckless Dynasty #9 (Jodie & Toby)

Dark Halloween Knight (Calli & Batman)

Dark Knight #10 (Calli & Batman)

Dark Princess #11 (Calli & Batman)

Dark Legacy #12 (Calli & Batman)

Corrupt Valentine Knight (Nico & Siren)

Ruined Series

Ruined Plans #1

Ruined by Lies #2

Ruined Promises #3

Never Forget Series

Never Forget Him #1

Never Forget Us #2

Everywhere & Nowhere #3

Chasing Series

Chasing Logan

The Cocktail Girls

His Manhattan

Her Kensington

SNEAK PEEK

THORN is my newly released high school bully romance. Check out a sneak peek!

THORN - CHAPTER ONE
AMALIE

"I think you'll really enjoy your time here," Principal Hartmann says. He tries to sound cheerful about it, but he's got sympathy oozing from his wrinkled, tired eyes.

This shouldn't have been part of my life. I should be in London starting university, yet here I am at the beginning of what is apparently my junior year at an American high school I have no idea about aside from its name and the fact my mum attended many years ago. A lump climbs up my throat as thoughts of my parents hit me without warning.

"I know things are going to be different and you might feel that you're going backward, but I can assure you it's the right thing to do. It will give you the time you need to... adjust and to put some serious thought into what you want to do once you graduate."

Time to adjust. I'm not sure any amount of time will be enough to learn to live without my parents and being shipped across the Pacific to start a new life in America.

"I'm sure it'll be great." Plastering a fake smile on my face, I take the timetable from the principal's hand and stare down at it. The butterflies that were already fluttering around in my stomach erupt to the point I might just throw up over his chipped Formica desk.

Math, English lit, biology, gym, my hands tremble until I see something that instantly relaxes me, *art and film studies.* At least I got my own way with something.

"I've arranged for someone to show you around. Chelsea is the captain of the cheer squad, what she doesn't know about the school isn't worth knowing. If you need anything, Amalie, my door is always open."

Nodding at him, I rise from my chair just as a soft knock sounds out and a cheery brunette bounces into the room. My knowledge of American high schools comes courtesy of the hours of films I used to spend my evenings watching, and she fits the stereotype of captain to a tee.

"You wanted something, Mr. Hartmann?" she sings so sweetly it makes even my teeth shiver.

"Chelsea, this is Amalie. It's her first day starting junior year. I trust you'll be able to show her around. Here's a copy of her schedule."

"Consider it done, sir."

"I assured Amalie that she's in safe hands."

I want to say it's my imagination but when she turns her big chocolate eyes on me, the light in them diminishes a little.

"Lead the way." My voice is lacking any kind of enthusiasm and from the narrowing of her eyes, I don't think she misses it.

I follow her out of the room with a little less bounce in my step. Once we're in the hallway, she turns her eyes on me. She's really quite pretty with thick brown hair, large eyes, and full lips. She's shorter than me, but then at five foot eight, you'll be hard pushed to find many other teenage girls who can look me in the eye.

Tilting her head so she can look at me, I fight my smile. "Let's make this quick. It's my first day of senior year and I've got shit to be doing."

Spinning on her heels, she takes off and I rush

to catch up with her. "Cafeteria, library." She points then looks down at her copy of my timetable. "Looks like your locker is down there." She waves her hand down a hallway full of students who are all staring our way, before gesturing in the general direction of my different subjects.

"Okay, that should do it. Have a great day." Her smile is faker than mine's been all morning, which really is saying something. She goes to walk away, but at the last minute turns back to me. "Oh, I forgot. That over there." I follow her finger as she points to a large group of people outside the open double doors sitting around a bunch of tables. "That's *my* group. I should probably warn you now that you won't fit in there."

I hear her warning loud and clear, but it didn't really need saying. I've no intention of befriending the cheerleaders, that kind of thing's not really my scene. I'm much happier hiding behind my camera and slinking into the background.

Chelsea flounces off and I can't help my eyes from following her out toward *her* group. I can see from here that it consists of her squad and the football team. I can also see the longing in other student's eyes as they walk past them. They either want to be them or want to be part of their stupid little gang.

Jesus, this place is even more stereotypical than I was expecting.

Unfortunately, my first class of the day is in the direction Chelsea just went. I pull my bag up higher on my shoulder and hold the couple of books I have tighter to my chest as I walk out of the doors.

I've not taken two steps out of the building when my skin tingles with awareness. I tell myself to keep my head down. I've no interest in being their entertainment but my eyes defy me, and I find myself looking up as Chelsea points at me and laughs. I knew my sudden arrival in the town wasn't a secret. My mum's legacy is still strong, so when they heard the news, I'm sure it was hot gossip.

Heat spreads from my cheeks and down my neck. I go to look away when a pair of blue eyes catch my attention. While everyone else's look intrigued, like they've got a new pet to play with, his are haunted and angry. Our stare holds, his eyes narrow as if he's trying to warn me of something before he menacingly shakes his head.

Confused by his actions, I manage to rip my

eyes from his and turn toward where I think I should be going.

I only manage three steps at the most before I crash into something—or somebody.

"Shit, I'm sorry. Are you okay?" a deep voice asks. When I look into the kind green eyes of the guy in front of me, I almost sigh with relief. I was starting to wonder if I'd find anyone who wasn't just going to glare at me. I know I'm the new girl but shit. They must experience new kids on a weekly basis, I can't be that unusual.

"I'm fine, thank you."

"You're the new British girl. Emily, right?"

"It's Amalie, and yeah... that's me."

"I'm so sorry about your parents. Mom said she was friends with yours." Tears burn my eyes. Today is hard enough without the constant reminder of everything I've lost. "Shit, I'm sorry. I shouldn't have—"

"It's fine," I lie.

"What's your first class?"

Handing over my timetable, he quickly runs his eyes over it. "English lit, I'm heading that way. Can I walk you?"

"Yes." His smile grows at my eagerness and for

the first time today my returning one is almost sincere.

"I'm Shane, by the way." I look over and smile at him, thankfully the hallway is too noisy for us to continue any kind of conversation.

He seems like a sweet guy but my head's spinning and just the thought of trying to hold a serious conversation right now is exhausting.

Student's stares follow my every move. My skin prickles as more and more notice me as I walk beside Shane. Some give me smiles but most just nod in my direction, pointing me out to their friends. Some are just downright rude and physically point at me like I'm some fucking zoo animal awoken from its slumber.

In reality, I'm just an eighteen-year-old girl who's starting somewhere new, and desperate to blend into the crowd. I know that with who I am—or more who my parents were—that it's not going to be all that easy, but I'd at least like a chance to try to be normal. Although I fear I might have lost that the day I lost my parents.

"This is you." Shane's voice breaks through my thoughts and when I drag my head up from avoiding everyone else around me, I see he's holding the door open.

Thankfully the classroom's only half full, but still, every single set of eyes turn to me.

Ignoring their attention, I keep my head down and find an empty desk toward the back of the room.

Once I'm settled, I risk looking up. My breath catches when I find Shane still standing in the doorway, forcing the students entering to squeeze past him. He nods his head. I know it's his way of asking if I'm okay. Forcing a smile onto my lips, I nod in return and after a few seconds, he turns to leave.

THORN - CHAPTER TWO
JAKE

"I don't see what the big deal is," Chelsea whines to her friends. "She's not even really that pretty. Look." I can't help but follow her finger as she points across the quad. My eyes find the tall blonde girl immediately. My lips press into a thin line and my blood boils. Feelings that I've fought for years to keep locked down threaten to bubble up.

Ripping my eyes away, I stare down at the bench below me. My heart races and my vision blurs. Suddenly, I'm a six-year-old boy again watching my world fall apart.

The girls continue bitching but I zone them out, too lost in my own turmoil to care about their pathetic opinions on the looks of the new girl. She won't fit in here. I'm going to make damn sure of it.

"I have no idea what they're chatting about. She is fine with a capital F," Mason, my best friend says, his stare still focused on the blonde everyone seems so fascinated with.

"She ain't all that."

"What the fuck is wrong with you? It's the first day of senior year, it doesn't get any better than this."

"If you say so. I'm outta here."

"Jake, hold up."

I ignore him and jump from the bench. I must only make it two steps when a gasp makes me look up. When I do, I watch as New Girl collides with Shane, one of our players. His hands grip onto her upper arms to steady her. The sight of him touching her, protecting her has fire erupting inside of me. Just looking at her makes me feel vulnerable, and that's not something I ever want to experience again.

"What's going on?" Mason and Ethan flank my sides and stare at the same car crash that I am.

"You calling her?" Ethan asks, following my stare.

Not having a fucking care in the world has resulted in one thing at least. My reputation. I do what the fuck I like, when I like and everyone around here knows it's best to just let me do my thing. That means not turning up to class, getting off my ass drunk, and most importantly, I get first pick of the girls. The others can have her once I'm done if they like, I don't care about passing them down once I'm done. But I never get sloppy seconds. Ever.

"She's off limits."

"I fucking knew you wanted her," Ethan mocks before I turn and fist his shirt. The blood drains from his face as he prepares for the hit he's expecting.

"I don't fucking want her. I'm saying she's off fucking limits. You got that?"

"Yeah-yeah. Off limits, got it."

"And make sure everyone fucking knows it. That bitch don't belong here and we're about to show her."

"Are we done here?" Mason asks. He's always been the slightly cooler headed one out of the three of us. He pulls my arm away from Ethan and steps between us, but not before a confused look passes between the two of them.

Staking claim on a girl isn't unusual, but what I just did. That shit isn't normal and without intending to, I just showed both of them a side of me that I don't want anyone to ever witness. Weakness.

"Are you sure everything's all right?" Mason asks once again when we fall into step in the direction of our first class.

"Yeah. Just feeling the pressure, I guess."

"This year's gonna be great."

Raising an eyebrow at him, I wait for him to explain how that's going to happen. Rosewood High's football team has never been all that. We have all the passion and dedication we need, but historically, it doesn't help all that much. Every year Coach gives the speech that this year is going to be the year but as of yet, we've never progressed more than a few games into the state playoffs. I can admit that our team is performing better than ever, but I don't want to set my hopes on anything epic.

For me, football's a release. A way to work out the tension and to forget about my bullshit life. I might give it my all, but I'm under no illusion that it's my life. Some of the guys have high hopes of getting scouted for college and I'm sure for a few of them it'll happen but I doubt we'll ever see their names on the NFL team sheets.

"Don't give me that look, Thorn. You know as well as I do that this is our year. With you in charge, there's no way we won't make it to the end."

I can't criticize his enthusiasm, that's for sure. It's just a shame I don't feel it. And *her* arrival sure isn't going to help matters.

DOWNLOAD NOW to continue reading.

www.ingramcontent.com/pod-product-compliance
Lightning Source LLC
Chambersburg PA
CBHW061547210726
48287CB00006B/2102